Also by Robert Coover

The Origin of the Brunists

The Universal Baseball Association,
J. Henry Waugh, Prop.

Pricksongs & Descants (short fiction)

A Theological Position (plays)

The Public Burning

A Political Fable

Spanking the Maid

Gerald's Party

A Night at the Movies (short fiction)

WHATEVER HAPPENED

—— TO ——

GLOOMY GUS

—— OF THE ——

CHICAGO BEARS?

ROBERT COOVER

The Linden Press/Simon and Schuster
New York 1987

A shorter version of this work originally appeared in
American Review 22.

Published by The Linden Press/Simon and Schuster
A Division of Simon & Schuster, Inc.
Simon & Schuster Building
Rockefeller Center
1230 Avenue of the Americas
New York, New York 10020
THE LINDEN PRESS/SIMON AND SCHUSTER
and colophon are trademarks of Simon & Schuster, Inc.
Designed by Anne Scatto/Levavi & Levavi
Manufactured in the United States of America
1 3 5 7 9 10 8 6 4 2
Library of Congress Cataloging-in-Publication Data
Coover, Robert.
Whatever happened to Gloomy Gus of the
Chicago Bears?

"Revised edition of a work originally published
in a different form"—Verso t.p.
I. Title.
PS3553.0633W4   1987   813'.54   87–2722
ISBN: 0–671–63813–0

For Pili:
May there always be
one more anniversary . . .

It's the Duke of Windsor's wedding day. $1300 worth of flowers have arrived at their French château to "festoon the nuptials," while back home in Baltimore, we're told, Mrs. Simpson's house is being reopened as a shrine and museum. EDWARD BOSSES WALLY AROUND AND SHE LIKES IT. She's in fluted blue today with a bonnet of feathers and tulle. Elsewhere, another Soviet marshal is being shot, a young American is being guillotined in Fascist Germany for plotting against anti-Semites, a supposed has-been named Bill Dietrich pitched a no-hitter for the White Sox, and up in Wisconsin some guy dynamited his whole family just "because they wouldn't help around the farm." And here in Chicago Gloomy Gus is dead. I walk home from the county hospital, through the cool rain, up Ogden, thinking: Only for the egoist and the dogmatist (and maybe they're one and the same, although I'm thinking of two different friends of mine) is there one "history" only. The rest of us live with the suspicion that there are as many histories as there are people and maybe a few more—out here in the flood, after all (I chuck the day-old *Trib* in a bin as I pass), what arrangements can we *not* imagine? Of course, we share some of the same information, call it that—Gus, for example, is dead in all our histories—but it's never enough to call "History." What do we have? Births, debts, deaths, and the weather.

Which as usual in Chicago is pretty grim. I'm getting soaked through, but to tell the truth, I don't mind the rain—it's been too hot, we all need the cooling off. It's about the best news we've got, in fact, possibly excepting that of Mrs. Simpson's festooned nuptials. I'm grateful just for the physical contact. Watching life vanish, even from a punch-drunk loony like Gloomy Gus, has a way of disconnecting me from things, and the cold wet wind blowing in off Lake Michigan, down Ogden's diagonal swath and into my face, helps put my feet back on the streets again. I might even be able to go home and weld another piece on Maxim Gorky's nose, I think. His nose is broad and generous: yes, maybe I can work again, why not? Gus is dead, Leo's left town, Maxie is on his way to Spain, O.B. to New York, maybe I can clear the rest of those bums out of my studio and get some work done. I need to be cut off for a while, need to think out my half-formed plan to follow Maxie to Spain. If I could only finish the Gorky. Then I could go and die and feel less guilty about it.

Poor old Gus was the eleventh fatality from Sunday's confrontation down at Republic Steel, most of them shot in the back; hundreds more were wounded and bashed, and now Kelly's cops, not merely exonerated but eulogized for their wholesale shooting and clubbing of unarmed workers (okay, they weren't all workers), have been given open license to hunt down all "agitators." Which can mean just about anyone they and the strikebreaker gangs choose it to mean: RIOTS BLAMED ON RED CHIEFS. I suppose, in the general—and willful—confusion, that might even, ironically, include me. It's Haymarket Square all over again, Chicago's old conspiracy called law and order. Hystereotypical, man, as O.B. would say. Still, it's not the '20s, I shouldn't let myself sink into Leo's cynicism. Things are changing. It's no longer a capital crime to belong to a union, and there've been real victories, most recently General Motors and Chrysler and U.S. Steel, Leo's been part of them. The Wagner Act got past the Supreme Court just this past month, union organizers are guests of Congress, even the chaingangs have been put on forty-four-hour weeks, it's a new world. Sure it is, I can hear him laugh sourly, but nudge the establishment, Meyer, and you can still get killed in it.

It was Leo who took Gus down to the Memorial Day demonstration Sunday. What had he intended? With Leo you could never be sure. Much less Gus, the poor freak. Whether he was trying to put on an entertainment for that cop, tackle him, or hump him, we'll never know. Whichever, or all three, or something else, there's no doubt he was caught offside once again and for the last time, his original sin. But he went down with real style and a complete disregard for his own skin, exemplifying a remark he once made to a sports reporter after a tough game: "A man is not afraid at a time like this because he blocks out any thought of fear by a conscious act of will. He concentrates entirely on the problem which faces him and forgets about himself." Inarticulate as he was, where did Gus find these words? In books? From other interviews? Was he coached? Or maybe he didn't say it, maybe some reporter made it up. As for the cop, when they told him it was the famous Chicago Bears halfback he'd shot, all he could do was stammer lamely that he was a Cubs fan.

There's a line in Gorky's *My Universities:* "I noticed—how many times?—that everything unusual and phantastical, however far from the truth it might be—appeals to people much more than serious stories of actual life." Maybe this is because, in the end, the "phantastical" stories are easier to believe. Leo told me recently that one of the Syn-

dicate's booming operations these days is the sup-
plying of weapons to both sides in industrial dis-
putes: blackjacks, billyclubs, firearms, steel bars,
baseball bats, charged wires, and steam lines, even
ax handles never made for axes. He said that Republic Steel has bought ten times as many gas guns
and twenty-five times as many gas shells and pro-
jectiles over the past three or four years as the
whole city of Chicago, and claimed they recruit
their scabs direct from the underworld. He was
telling me this to explain why the union needed its
own arsenal, whatever the source, its own army of
volunteers. "Workers aren't warriors," he's often
said. "In armed conflict, you need some pros." Not
that the unions do much recruiting from the underworld, of course. "Those guys are instinctively re-
actionary, the boss-pool you might call them, you
can't trust them." I'm sure the regret in his voice
was sincere. And then that mustachioed grin: "Now,
psychos, on the other hand . . ." I find it hard to
cope with this realism. "As a socialist, Meyer," Simon likes to say, "you'd make a good gardener."
This is true. I think of myself as a lyrical socialist,
which makes about as much sense, given the world
we live in, as being an anal-retentive anarchist with
a bomb in his hand. Leo, it goes without saying,
disappeared right after the riot. "If they ask where
I am," he told me on the phone, "tell them I've
gone to Spain to get killed." Which was not so

much information as a dig at me. I supposed he was actually across the line somewhere on his way to one of Girdler's other steel mills in Ohio or Michigan—Canton maybe, he might have been trying to give me a hint: mostly immigrant Spaniards there, after all, an unstable mix of anarchists and socialists with ties still to their suicidally warring movements back home in the Republic.

Spain's a good place to go to get killed, all right, Leo's right about that. Or mutilated: they say that three quarters of all the volunteers who've gone over there are already dead or wounded. Fascist propaganda maybe—but what would I do without my arms? or my eyes? Crossing the railroad line, I find myself for the first time in over a month crawling down by the tracks in what was once an old habit, scratching about in the light rain for iron spikes and nails lying loose. It wouldn't be a surprise, I think, feeling the tenderness in my blackened eye like a word of advice, to find out that the Abraham Lincoln Battalion is being financed by rightwing industrialists in this country like Tom Girdler, happy to rid themselves once and for all of indigenous romantics. Spain: the new Hog Butcher of the World. Am I really going to follow Maxie over there? Since the bombing of Guernica a little over a month ago, I've felt I had to go, that I'd never work again until I did, but now, hunkered down beside these gleaming wet rails stretching off subversively into the tunneled distance and feeling no pull on me, no pull at all, I'm not so sure. Behind me, back down Ogden, is the old neighborhood with its street garbage and hangouts, the Russishe shul, Central Hebrew High, the gangfights outside Davy Miller's, the horseradish grinders and umbrella men with their crude jokes, my uncle's humid laundry business, the old people's home where he died complaining about the bills, "Oi, vai! A sof! A sof!" I've been running from that all these years. Out of the neighborhood, out of the city, away from the state, across the country, headed for Mexico at one time, dreaming even of Palestine, Maxie's big goal. Now here I am, still on its short leash. It has taken me a long time to come home: am I going to leave it again? Yet can I do otherwise? If my country would say yes, if it would ask me to go, it would be so much easier. Maybe then I'd even feel less like an exile. The spikes are beautiful: hand-hammered, square, little sculptures on their own. I pocket a handful of them ("Can we just sit here in Chicago," Maxie demanded—and he wasn't declaiming, it was an expression from the heart—"and let such things happen? Will we do nothing to stop this evil?"), as well as some small gears, some brass moldings, and what looks like a distributor baseplate. There's also an apple lying there, partly eaten ("It is like a sickness spreading into the world—and where, if not there, will the line be drawn?"); I was glad I didn't have to pick it up.

I've not worked since the bombing of Guernica five weeks ago, haven't even been contributing my share to the WPA project. Which I like: a park sculpture meant as a clambering device for little kids. But there was a park in Guernica too, kids playing. The German Condor Legion hit the town on market day, nowhere to hide, thousands of people killed and torn apart, cremated in the fires that followed. It was a completely inhuman thing, and it made me a little crazy. Of course, the world is full of sadness—all the massacres in Spain, in Ethiopia, in China, here in this country for that matter: men tortured with blowtorches, then hung from trees and set alight—but this was something new. Others could put a good face on it, talk about its arousing world opinion finally against the Fascist terror—how could Roosevelt ignore *this?*—but I felt like those people out on the Caspian steppes must have felt all those centuries ago, ancestors of mine maybe, when they first saw those strange monsters thundering down on them from the morning sun, awesome, dismaying (the rumble of it, the precision, the terror)—no, not the Mongols, hordes like any hordes, but the *horses*. Now I look up in the sky, where life comes from, and see it dark, yet garish, ablaze with metallic death.

I destroyed half a year's labors that afternoon in

a fit of—what? despair? guilt? outrage? revelation? childish nihilism? I don't know. All I remember is I picked up the oxyacetylene torch as the news came through on the radio, in between soap commercials, thinking to fight back with art, to forge some affirmation in the face of so much annihilation, something like that, and instead I went berserk, fusing everything within the blowpipe's reach, including a stack of metal folding chairs, the pipe on my old stove, and the bars at the foot of my iron bed. In fact, it was the alarming stench of burning blankets and mattress straw that finally brought me back to my senses—I twisted the valves shut, threw a pot of cold coffee at the smoldering bedding, wrenched the sagging bars at the foot upright and held them till they cooled, and then fell down on the bed, still in my gloves and goggles, to lie in all that stink and wreckage, thinking: This is probably more or less what the survivors of Guernica are doing, because: what else can they do? I stared at the melted cityscapes, the mowed Jarama flowers, the broken-backed jugglers. A cat made of little pennyworth nails I'd been working on for nearly a year had collapsed on its own fused belly like an old drunk. Nearly a year! What have I been doing all this time? I must be mad!

The Black Baron wandered in then, looking faintly offended, circled the bed once, then jumped up beside me. "Baron," I said, "Leo's right. Art's just another form of hysteria. If you're not on the front lines, you're dead." The Baron purred. "We've got to grow up, Baron. We've got to learn how to kill." Instead, though, I dropped off into a deep thick begoggled sleep . . . from which—only today, it might be said—I'm at last stirring. . . .

At the river, where it rolls under Ogden, I pause, watching the rain freckle the dirty brown water, sweeping back and forth with the wind like indefatigable and ever renewable armies. An illusion, of course. Armies can perish entirely, causes can be lost, nothing is inevitable. Just because people can control their thoughts, they suppose they can control the world of things. They project their convictions out on the world and are surprised when the world takes no notice. A kind of magical thinking: Freud called it "omnipotence of thoughts." I've often been guilty of it myself in that space of time between thinking up a new idea for a sculpture and actually picking up the torch to begin. All the worse when it happens out in the world. Orthodox Marxists like my friend Simon tend to forget the old rabbi's warning—"History is *nothing but* the activity of man pursuing his aims"—and to look upon history not as the minute-by-minute invention it really is, but as a kind of discovery, something that unfolds inexorably before your eyes, in

19

spite of all of man's willful and unwillful resistance. Which is, as Leo puts it, a lot of mystical borax. Nothing so infuriates Leo as Simon saying something like "You can't hurry history, comrade." Usually, this is Simon's excuse for avoiding demonstrations and the like, and so that makes Leo all the madder. "Listen, Simon," he'll yell, his mustaches bristling, "I don't believe in historical forces and I don't believe in moral positions. Nobody's got a right to anything, and nothing—*nothing*, goddamn it!—is inexorable. The struggle against oppression seems endless, but it can end, and the oppression is real but it is not immoral. I can understand these shits like Girdler. If I'd inherited a railroad or a steel plant, or had fought my way up the goddamn ladder like he did to get one, I'd be on the other side fighting to keep what I had, just as hard as I'm fighting now to take it away. Partly just because it's *fun*. And don't think any crazy historical spirit or supposedly superior morality would stop me! All that's just fiction, brother, and fiction is the worst enemy we got!"

Leo's right when he argues that actions are the only hard things in the world—I also believe in the essential softness of objects, the hardness of gesture, it's why I like to work in welded metal. But these actions have less certain meaning and more lives in the world than Leo likes to allow, and he's too much gripped by the image of life as a gutter fight. Of course, the Party's doing everything it can to make it seem like one since the Stalin–Trotsky split, turning old family friends like Simon and Harry into mortal enemies, and the kangaroo trials in Russia right now are making Leo's claim that "the only real joy in life is power, and there's just not enough of it to go around," sound like a truism, but this is to ignore the effect a changed context can have and to underestimate the appetite for hope and brotherhood. Leo also finds my jugglers and athletes frivolous, but that's because he talks without listening to himself; he'd be much closer to the mark to say they were self-contradictory. Leo puts a lot of people off with his hardnosed bluster, but I've always felt close to him. He and Jesse befriended me during rough times on the road, and I followed them around in their efforts to organize coal miners, tenant farmers, ironworkers, housewreckers, Leo becoming a kind of father figure to me. Not having had one of my own. And from those times, I know that Leo's not the cynic he pretends to be. If anything, he's too ruled by his emotions. Injustice offends him at some level that seems almost organic, and he stakes out these skeptical positions to give himself more room to move and breathe.

I pick up a broken chip of concrete and toss it idly into the river, meaning nothing by it, except maybe as a kind of calendar notation. It occurs to me that Leo would have looked for a boulder, Jesse would have tried to skip the thing, Golda would have loved the chip and grieved when it was gone. Gus? Probably he'd have carried it into the river on an end run. Or delivered Hamlet's soliloquy to it as to Yorick's skull. Though on the night we showed his talents off to Leo, I should say, he gave no sign of knowing *Hamlet*—or even of its existence. By then I knew a lot of the plays he'd been in, and so got him to do Aeneas for us, the prosecuting attorney from *The Night of January 16th* and the greenhorn playwright from *The Dark Tower.* Leo was particularly impressed by a bit Gus did from an unknown one-acter called *The Price of Coal,* and the old innkeeper's weeping scene from *Bird-in-Hand,* which, in spite of its feudal sentiments (the thrust of the play is the old man's opposition to his daughter's marrying into the upper classes: "And we've always known 'oo was 'oo and which 'at fitted which 'ead . . ."), was very moving. Tears actually welled up in his eyes and rolled down his cheeks into his black beard when he reached the lines: "H' I'm sorry about wot h' I've done tonight. H' I shall be sorry for h' it till the end of me life. H' I've be'ayved so as h' I ought to be h' ashamed, h' I know. But this business"—*sob!*—" 'as pretty near broke me 'eart . . . !"

"Jesus, that's terrific!" Leo laughed. We got Gus to repeat it a couple of times to show Leo how the

22

tears fell right on cue each time through. "Hey, brother, I could use you down at the steel mill next week!" Leo said, half jokingly, yet clearly considering the possibilities at the same time. When I tried to caution him, he wouldn't listen, so I shouted out: "*29!*" Gus jumped to his feet, ducked his head down into his shoulders, and—*wham!*—piled into my potbellied stove. Luckily, there was no fire in it, or he'd have been badly burnt. As it was, there was a tremendous crash of stovepipe, grates, and dishes, cinders and coaldust flying everywhere, and a big hole in the partition between my room and the studio out front. "Holy shit!" Leo gasped. "This guy's a fucking tornado!" My intention had been to convince Leo not to take Gus down to the Memorial Day demonstration ("More like the *Hindenburg,*" I suggested), but I apparently accomplished just the opposite. It hasn't escaped me that I am, indirectly anyway, responsible for Gus's death.

Not his real name, of course. He picked it up back in college when he was still playing freshman football—or trying to—for the Whittier Poets. When he joined the Chicago Bears, sportswriters started calling him the Fighting Quaker and, for reasons never quite clear to me (maybe it had something to do with his battering-ram style of running), Iron Butt, but Gloomy Gus was the name that stuck to him. Not because he was actually a gloomy sort of character—I doubt he had any feelings at all, as we know them anyway, he wasn't put together that way—but because it was a clown's name, and a clown was what Gus was, even when he was a National Hero. He was the most famous guy I ever knew—a college All-American and an all-star football pro—and, as such, a kind of walking cautionary tale on the subject of fame and ambition.

He first turned up at a party we threw in my studio one Friday toward the end of March, and he came back every Friday night after. "A f'kucken schnorrer," Harry called him, "f'kucken" being his own Yiddish-American neologism, made of *kucken*, fucking, and *fehkuckteh*, but Gus wasn't there to sponge exactly. It was just his style: everything by the numbers, one to ten and start again. In fact, he was one of the hardest workers I ever knew. Maybe that was why they called him Iron Butt, I don't know. Jesse speculated it had to do with his Bear teammates' inability to crack his virginity in the lockerrooms; he made up a funny song about it, a parody of "John Henry" in which the steel-drivin' man meets his match at last. Gus was a strange guest, my principal distraction through the hands-down melancholy of this past month, but maybe he contributed to it, too. He ate my food, drank the Baron's milk, crapped in my toilet, washed in my basin, even used my bed, but never a word of thanks, not even the least sign that he understood these things were mine and not his. Simon joked he was just being a good comrade, true to the canons, but then Gus wasn't mooching off Simon. In place of thanks, we got performances. Sometimes by request, sometimes spontaneous, but never entirely predictable. He'd laid on several skills in his lifetime, and he didn't always come up with the right ones in the right order.

I hadn't recognized him at first, which is not surprising, since not only had he been wearing a bushy black beard and been introduced as an actor living off the WPA like the rest of us, but I wouldn't ordinarily recognize any professional football player, by face or name, nor would any of my friends. Of course I like the game—I like all games—but I don't keep up with the overblown seasonal histories. Nevertheless, it happens that I did know who Gloomy Gus was, had even for a few weeks a couple of years back followed his then-fabulous career, and I eventually put two and two together (the answer in Gus's case was not four, not even close), though I admit I got some help from visitors who came through asking about him.

That time when I was reading about him was the autumn of 1934. I'd come back to Chicago after a couple of years bumming around, following the harvests and the unionizing. I was tired of that life and wanted to get back to sculpting again. I'd learned a new skill on the road, welding, and I

knew at last where I was going, if I could ever get
the money together for a studio and equipment. I was
staying at that time down on Kedzie with my aunt.
I had no place to begin work, so I took a refresher
course in plumbing and metalworking at the Jewish Training School and spent the rest of my time
reading. Anything at hand, which at my aunt's
house was mostly mystical tracts and newspapers.
And the papers that fall were full of the incredible
exploits of Gloomy Gus of the Chicago Bears. It
was his rookie season in the bigtime and he was
breaking every record in the books, just as he had
done in college ball. The reporters were so excited
it was sometimes hard to tell the newspapers from
the mystical tracts. I read that he'd played for a
little Quaker school out in California, and had set
phenomenal rushing, passing, pass-receiving, and
scoring records—including seven touchdowns, almost single-handed (he was always a loner, and
besides, nobody else was really good enough to
keep up with him) against Pittsburgh in the Rose
Bowl. There was even a popular song about him,
"You Gotta Be a Football Hero." He was everybody's All-American, and all the big professional
teams were after him. He wasn't interested in the
negotiations apparently, and would have played
for nothing (though this may have been some publicity tararam handed out by the Bears' front office), but he was very loyal to all his friends and

relatives, his old coach, former teammates and girl-friends, and so the price was finally pretty high, especially considering the hard times. Since the Bears were the reigning league champions and had all the money, they were the ones who got him. And it was worth it, or so it seemed that fall: he led the Bears to a perfect season in the conference—thirteen wins, no ties, no losses—and again completely rewrote the record books. Only in the last game or two did the cracks begin to show, but before the playoff for the championship with the New York Giants had ended, his legendary career was over. Until then, he'd been living the dream of every little school kid in America: the quiet scholarly little boy, left out of all the neighborhood games and laughed at by all the girls, who suddenly finds the magic formula and becomes the most famous athlete and greatest lover in the world. "I believe in the American dream," he once said, "because I have seen it come true in my own life."

I'm just crossing Division Street when I run into my friend Jesse, coming out of a bar with Harry and Ilya. Ilya I haven't seen in weeks. He's very drunk and sullen—a pale wispy boy who never looks quite strong enough to stand, even when he's sober. His brother Dave, we learned a couple of weeks ago, lost an arm and part of a leg at Jarama—like Ilya, he's a musician: a violinist, was—and since then Ilya's become secretive and ill-tempered, almost as though he somehow blamed the rest of us for what happened to his brother. He still looks that way, though that he's out drinking with Jesse and Harry is a good sign. Leo had once, soberly, more or less soberly, lectured me on alcohol and revolution, the link being the romantic illusion. "And why not?" he'd grinned wearily (we were watching drunken Father Clanahan tip over, as I recall). "Reality's such shit. You have to reinvent it just to live in it." "Hey, Meyer!" Jesse calls now, flashing his lean, gap-toothed smile from under his rumpled cloth cap. "How's ole Gus?"

"He died."

Jesse and Harry somehow look downcast and amused at the same time. The momentary fade Jesse passes into suggests he's already conjuring up a new song. Come all you good workers, a story I will tell, about a football hero who for our Union fell. Ilya, who introduced Gus to us in the first place, only grimaces irritably and looks down at his feet. "The silly potz," Harry sighs, shaking his little round head. Harry was always baffled by Gus, and has never got over his rage at what Gus did to his sister. "Was he still taking curtain calls at the end?"

"No," I say, "though he had an audience—the place was filled with celebrities and reporters. But he didn't seem to recognize them. He just lay there, like he didn't know what was happening. They'd shaved his beard off, and it made him look puffy and gray and vulnerable."

"This is the city of the gray faces," says Harry cryptically, squinting up at us through the rain streaking his thick smudged lenses. Harry is a poet and a Trotskyite, and he loves enigma.

Jesse glances at Ilya, then explains: "Harry 'n me been down to the Eagles on Houston where they got those fellas laid out. Huge crowds down there, Meyer, like you never seen, folks payin' their respecks from all over the country." He shakes his head, a flash of bitterness sobering the

29

genial creases of his face. "At least seven a them boys, you know, got it in the back."

"So I heard. Our brave boys in blue."

"It was sad to see, Meyer. Them fellas is completely dead. And a lotta others are hurtin', too. The hall down there had the ass-pick of a first-aid shelter in a fuckin' war zone." Jesse cups his big hands against the rain and lights a cigarette, watching Ilya, a sincere worry on his face. "Crushed skulls, broke ribs, 'n suchlike," he says around the smoke. "Seen a pore woman who's gone stone blind, her head fulla stitches like the goddamn Bride a Frankenstein. An' a guy with a bullet hole clean through his left flapper, talkin' about how lucky he was."

Ilya snorts, staring at the traffic in the street behind me. "Lucky!"

"They even wounded a little kid," says Harry, his gray jowls puffy with indignation. "A little petseleh not more than nine, they were shooting at everybody. And an expectant mother. Just missed killing the bloody foetus—and they won't even let her out of jail!"

"It's true," Jesse says. "A dude was locked up with me all night who'd been shot in the leg. His wounds was festerin' up 'n he was gittin' feverish, but they wouldn't let him go. Hell, no. Far as I know, the pore sonuvabitch is dead by now. An' the damn cops is talkin' like they cain't wait to shoot some more. But nobody's scared, that's the main thing you notice down there, they're jist mad." Jesse's theme song: the universal war. Which side are you on. Injustice is as plain as the nose on your face, you can't pretend you don't see it. Jesse's an old Wob, one of the few to stay with the union movement after the Wobblies fell apart, sweet but intransigent. He takes a deep drag on the cigarette, then hands it to Ilya. "Funny how the world works, you know. Seems like you always gotta go through flesh to git to the other side."

"You . . . !" growls Ilya, looking away but taking the smoke. Cars pass us in the street, a wet hum and throb.

Where Ilya reacted against the privileged survivors, hurting Jesse just a bit, I might have snorted at "the other side." Instead, I say: "Flesh isn't just a passive medium, you know. It talks back. Only sometimes in the excitement we forget to listen."

"Yeah, speakin' a that, ole son, howza mouse?" Jesse grins, peering closer.

"It's okay." I should be grateful for it, it may have saved my life. Because of it, Leo told me to stay home Sunday: they expected action, and the black eye would be too tempting a target. Badge of a troublemaker. Jesse missed the Memorial Day confrontation, too, having been arrested in a sound-truck on Wednesday as the men were first downing tools and coming out, released only yesterday.

"Seen Leo?" he asks now.

"He's left town."

"That figures," grumps Harry, who never went down to the strike at all. "He's a mamzer, a shvitser, you can't trust him."

"He's needed in Ohio," I say, defending my friend. "There's some kind of air war going on over there. Besides, he's a good organizer—"

"That patscher? He couldn't organize his rectum! He's a joyboy, Meyer, he's got no vision, no ideology, it's just a big circus to him. Look at him taking that dumb klutz down there Sunday! He knew f'kucken Karl Marx couldn't keep his signals straight, he *knew* what had to happen!"

"Turds like him are gonna get us all killed," grumbles Ilya, passing the cigarette back to Jesse. A bit unfair maybe, but at least it's a sign of health that he's said "us" again. Jesse winks soberly at me over the dangling butt.

"Maybe that wasn't a great idea," I admit. "But a lot of steelworkers are football fans. Leo thought that an expression of solidarity from a famous star like Gus could make a strong impression on them—"

"Well, it sure did that," agrees Harry. "It got ten of the poor shlimazels *killed!* It was that crazy charge on the police that set the whole meshugass off, I read it in the papers!"

"What paper wuzzat, comrade?" asks Jesse with a wry one-sided grin, and Harry grunts ambiguously.

"Leo told me Gus had nothing to do with it," I say. "He said it all started when some cop got nervous and shot into the crowd of workers crossing the field—then everybody just started running. Which is why so many of them got it in the back."

"If it *was* a cop," Jesse puts in. "Mighta been one of Girdler's comp'ny goons, tryin' to whup up a little action—we heard somethin' about that today down to the fun'ral."

"Maybe," I allow. "Wouldn't be the first time." Jesse nods. We're remembering Kansas, Pennsylvania, Kentucky. Bloody Thursday in San Francisco, where years ago we met. The cynical perverting of men's honest passions. "Anyway, Leo claims he tried to drag Gus away when the shooting broke out, but Gus seemed mesmerized by all the fireworks. You know what big crowds always did to him. Then some cop lobbed a gas grenade, Gus grabbed it in midair, and he was off and running. Jesse Owens couldn't catch him, Leo said. War Admiral couldn't. He said Gus sprinted the whole battle line between cops and workers, dodging clubs and stones and even bullets. A cop would be bashing a striker with a billy and Gus would time his run so as to go flashing between them on

33

the backswing, without even seeming to change his pace. That's real prairie out there, maybe the first time in years Gus had seen an open field, he was really moving." (On the phone, Leo had said: "For the first time I have to appreciate those welded bozos of yours, Meyer—do me one of that batbrain hauling his ashes through all that rowdy-dowdy, and you got yourself a patron! Ha ha! Even if I have to hock old Mother Blooey!" Meaning his car—named after the Grande Dame of the Party—his one possession.) "You're right about Leo never staying around when there's shooting going on, Harry," I add, "especially when it's all coming from one side, he wouldn't even argue with you about that, but he said he couldn't resist watching old Gloomy Gus make his fabulous run, even if it did mean he nearly got caught standing there. And the amazing thing was, Gus made it, juggling that smoking gas grenade, all the way from one end to the other!"

"Whoopee! What a way to go!" hoots Jesse, slapping his leg. He takes a final pleasurable pull, his pale blue eyes fixed remotely on Gus's run, and passes the butt between fingertips to Ilya. "Shit, boys, that musta been somethin' to see!" Yes, it's going to be a good song.

"Maybe those ten shmucks who got killed ran interference for him," suggests Harry sarcastically. "That's how many's on a football team, isn't it?"

Jesse laughs. "You think they were countin', Harry?"

"I heard a rumor down at the theater he might've been a police informer," Ilya says. We turn to watch him. He drops the butt, about the size of a used pencil eraser, onto the wet sidewalk and pointlessly steps on it, and as he does so seems to step into our circle. Or toward it anyway.

"What's that—?" asks Harry.

"You know, maybe the cops recognized him as one of their own pals and held their fire."

"No," I say, "they shot at him all right. At least according to what Leo says. In fact, before he got to the end, everybody was trying to get him, throwing or shooting whatever they had at him. He'd become like some kind of terrifying symbol or something, but they couldn't hit him. It was only when he'd finished his run and turned back to trot toward the cops with his arms stretched out in a V above his head that one of them shot him. This came as a complete surprise to him, of course. Leo says he just stood there, crumpling, that panicky twitching look in his face that always comes over him when he gets his signals crossed, and then the gas grenade blew up. That's when Leo said he left."

"A good story," harrumphs Harry. "Leo's still got his touch. But I don't believe it. Like my old bobbeh used to say, nisht geshtoigen, nisht gefloi-

35

gen—it don't stand, it don't fly. Except that part about Leo never staying around when the shooting starts. That had a ring of truth . . ."

"Whaddaya think about that rumor, Meyer?" Jesse asks. "What Ilya here was sayin'—you think ole Gus mighta been a Judas goat?"

"I don't know. That one was going around the hospital today, too. The cops weren't denying it, but maybe that's because they don't want to admit they've killed a famous middle-class hero. In fact, they were trying to suggest he might have been shot in the line of duty by one of the strikers, not by a cop at all, but not even the *Trib* seems to be buying that one."

"Still, think about it—he had all the gear, didn't he? Even a disguise! You always said he was like playactin' alla time, but he didn't seem to have no center. Maybe that was jist on accounta he couldn't *show* us the center . . ."

"Well . . ."

"Oi! it all fits!" cries Harry, slapping his round cheeks. "Why didn't we see it before? A f'kucken mosser! We're *all* geshtupped!"

"Maybe," I laugh, "but I doubt it. I like Leo's story better. Anyway, Leo's pretty sure we cleaned most of them out Friday and Saturday." I point to my eye and the others grin, all but Ilya, who seems unable to look at it.

"Hey, it's fucking cold and wet out here," he complains. "Let's get something to drink, goddamn it!"

Jesse grins and wraps a bony arm around him. "Wiser words, Ilya ole buddy," he says with a fake drunken slur, "was never spoke! C'mon, it's dog-fuckin' time, brothers!"

"Join us, Meyer," says Harry, searching for me through his thick wet glasses. "I'll buy you a glezel your Moldavskaya syrup."

"No, thanks. I'm going home and get some work done." They look surprised at this. I hope they'll take the hint. I'll start by repairing the cat, the one made of pennyworth nails. Find a place in it for one of these railroad spikes in my pocket. To prop up the fused belly, maybe. Scar tissue. "It's been awhile, you know . . ."

"Well, so that's good," says Harry, slapping my shoulder. He seems genuinely pleased. "Maybe we'll stop by later and see how it's going."

"Yeah, an', hey, pick me up somethin' cheap at Polly the Greek's, will ya, Meyer?" says Jesse, fishing for change. He drops a quarter in my hand, tips his long-billed cap, and they drift off, through the drizzle, stubby half-blind Harry, pale Ilya, and Jesse with his long skinny arms around the pair of them, singing snatches from Casey Bill's "WPA Blues"—

ROBERT COOVER

". . . Early next mornin' while I was
*   layin' in my bed,*
I heerd a mighty rumble of bricks comin'
*   down on my head,*
So I had to start duckin' and dodgin' and
*   be on my way,*
They was tearin' my house down on me—
That housewreckin' crew from the WPA!"

Jesse first sang us that song at the famous farewell party for Maxie in my studio back in March. It's strange to think how much everything's changed since then. That party was maybe the best one we've ever had. Sometimes I find it hard to believe in my own reality—the very idea of a conscious passage into and out of time seems like some kind of terrifying fairytale—but that night I felt very much at one with my own life and the lives of those around me. I even got a little drunk, unusual for me. My drinking habits are a kind of standing joke on Chicago's North Side, especially since my studio is an old plumbing supplies warehouse once used during Prohibition, according to local legend, as a clandestine liquor depot by Bugs Moran's gang. All I ever have is the occasional glass of sweet wine, the last vestige (I've thought until recently) of my rejected West Side childhood. That night I had several and soon became giddy and noisy in spite of myself, and I even danced a *kazatzke*. Or what I hoped passed for one, never having actually danced one before. Squatting and kicking the *prisiadka,* while the others clapped and chanted, I'd thought: *This* is what I've always wanted to do! Terrible sick hangover the next day—maybe we sweet-wine drinkers are the hardest and most self-punishing of all—but it was a small price to pay.

The party had been called with hardly any planning to celebrate the victory at Guadalajara and to say goodbye to Máxie. Maxie was on his way to join the Lincoln Battalion in Spain: he thought of it as a rite of passage on his route to Palestine. We all love and admire Maxie very much and were afraid for him, and hopeful. Ilya's brother David was already over there, crossing in the Christmas season with the first Americans to go, and our old West Coast CIO friends Eskill and Nicco and Richie as well. Many of us thought we'd be following. There was a real chance now. The Fascist advance had been stopped at last at the very edge of Madrid. We hadn't heard the worst about Jarama yet, didn't know that night that the untrained Lincolns had been almost wiped out in the mad attempt on Suicide Hill and were badly demoralized, didn't know that David had lost two of his limbs and that Nicco was dead, we only knew that the Americans had heroically held the line there against immeasurable odds: the Fascists did not pass. And now the greatest victory of the war: Mussolini's Blackshirt "volunteers"—there are said to be eighty thousand of them fighting for Franco in Spain, in spite of the so-called "Nonintervention Pact"—had been routed at Guadalajara, and in large part by their own countrymen, the famous Garibaldis of the International Brigade. The government counteroffensive, it was said, had begun. Newly trained Spanish divisions were being rushed to the front to replace the Italian Internationals. Russian tanks and guns had arrived, in fact they'd already helped win the battle at Guadalajara, and support from other countries like America, England, and France must not be far behind. It was in their own self-interest, after all. Roosevelt seemed to be hinting as much, and his new election mandate had freed him—indeed, *obliged* him—to act. Or anyway that's what we chose to believe that night. Many, unable to hear the awful afterclap of silence following Guernica, choose to believe it still. In the end it is, as it has no doubt always been, a naked contest between heart and steel. Must heart always win? Or rather: can it *ever* win? Leo laughs and says no, but that night he was a minority of one.

Though the Chicago weather was typically bitter, the studio was warm with the close press of friends, hot food and drink, music, good feelings. People wore ribbons and badges or pieces of clothing they associated with their Spanish brothers and sisters, and one of the women brought a big cake decorated with La Pasionaria's NO PASARÁN! The best was Thérèse, a wet nurse who'd helped lead a sit-down strike down at the Board of Health to get the price of her milk raised (they'd tried for ten cents an ounce, got four), who came dressed in a Flamenco dancer's costume fashioned entirely out of tissue paper, ribbons, and shredded Sears, Roebuck catalogues. "Whoo, it's really blowin' out there, honey!" she exclaimed breathlessly, fluttering in through the front door like a huge ruffled bird, snow capping her black brows, "I was dam' near gone with the wind!" I'd found a picture of Abraham Lincoln and had pasted up a large poster with a balloon coming out of Abe's mouth that read: VIVA LA QUINCE BRIGADA! Later, Leo laughed and called it jingoism, but we all laughed with him. The party was also for him and Jesse, as it turned out, and for the union victories in Michigan, a surprise homecoming—the sit-down strikes had done it. After a million dollars in private detectives and that much again in armaments, thugs, and counterpropaganda, General Motors and Chrysler had finally caved in and recognized the United Auto Workers. Leo and Jesse had come dashing straight back to the party from the mass rally in Detroit's Cadillac Square, skidding up to the curb outside in Mother Blooey, Leo's old beat-up Terraplane, and had rushed in to a burst of applause with three bottles of Old Quaker whiskey, a bucket of beans, and big placards that read SPIRIT OF 1937 and FORD TOMORROW!

It was Ilya who brought Gus along, introducing him as an actor in a WPA project that Ilya was composing a score for. It was a couple of weeks before we found out who he really was, and then thanks mainly to a reporter for the Hearst chain assigned to do a "Whatever Happened to ——?" story on him. I know people in the Theater Project—before I got reclassified as a sculptor last fall, I did set designs for the FTP—but when I asked Gus if he knew them, he only stared at me blankly. Well, it was a stupid question, one of those clinging rituals. I regretted it as soon as I'd asked it, and, smiling apologetically, led Gus over to the trestle table of food and drinks.

He was a bulky man—too bulky for an actor, I thought then, but later: rather small for a pro half-back—with a wide sloping nose, an intense but unfocused gaze, and a bushy black beard. "Hey, comrades! *It's f'kucken Karl Marx!*" Harry hollered drunkenly. Everybody laughed, but Harry couldn't have been further off the mark: Gus not only lacked political awareness, he lacked awareness of any kind. He had no core at all. Unless pure willpower has some kind of substance, amounts to some kind of character. We didn't discover this that night, of course, it took us awhile

43

to catch on to Gloomy Gus. But as we got to know him and something about his past—which was pretty remarkable in its way—it was this nothing-ness at the center that we all settled on as the essential Gloomy Gus. Ilya argued that it made him a good actor: the empty vessel. I disagreed. I don't believe in philosopher-actors any more than Ilya does, but skills alone aren't enough: good act-ors cannot merely *be* empty, they have to know how to *empty themselves*.

He was badly coordinated, too. The first two drinks we gave him slipped right through his hand and smashed on the floor. He didn't apologize, didn't pick up the broken glass, he just smiled va-cantly at us, waiting for another drink to be lodged in his still-cupped and outstretched hand. The third time, I propped an empty glass in his hands and made sure he had a grip on it before pouring—we'd had to scrape to get together what food and drink we had, and it hurt to waste any of it. "Tell me when," I said.

He stared at me searchingly, and after a mo-ment replied with boyish earnestness: "Honey, don't be impatient. The delay's been useful, hasn't it?"

"What—?!" I cried.

He became very jittery then, his eyes flicking from side to side as though deeply perplexed, hunting for something—then suddenly he seemed

to find it (I could almost hear the whirr-*click!*):
he smiled benignly, lovingly, and said in a deep
resonant voice: "Fannie, I ask you to marry me."

At first I though Ilya had put him up to it. But I
saw that Ilya was as amazed as I was. This guy
must be stewed, I thought. Or more likely: on
some kind of drugs. As it turned out, however,
these had been lines from two plays he'd been in—
The Dark Tower and *The Trysting Place* (I was
to get to know these plays all too well in the weeks
to follow)—and unwittingly I'd been throwing him
cues. He wasn't always like that, I should say.
Sometimes he was worse.

Sixty or seventy people turned up finally, filling
the place up. I was kept busy as the *de facto* host
and—purposely maybe (I was convinced by now
it was all a put-on, and felt I'd had my turn at
being the butt)—took little further notice of this
oddball actor, except to join him in the laughter
as he attempted clumsily, laboriously, mechani-
cally, but with farcical vehemence, to learn the
words to "The Internationale." It had started as
a mild taunt—"What kinda comrade actor are you,
Karl Marx," Harry had shouted good-naturedly, "if
you don't know 'The f'kucken Internationale'?"—
but it was like Harry had flicked a switch: Gus
looked up in alarm, blinked (we all laughed: he
was good at this, we felt), and commenced to struggle fiercely with the words of the song: "Arise ye,

uh, prisoners of starvation . . ." He became ob-
sessed by it, in fact—I caught glimpses of him
from time to time the rest of the night, off in some
corner of the studio, huddled among half-finished
creatures of mine (a lonely man at heart, I thought),
going over and over the lines: " 'Tis the final, uh,
conflict, Let each rise—no, stand . . ."

Though we didn't fully appreciate it at the time
(we still had a lot to learn about Gloomy Gus of
the Chicago Bears), Harry had done us all a favor,
keeping him at the edge of the party like that.
And I was granted my bountiful night, from which
sculptures have already flowed and can flow again,
if I can find my way back to the torch. People came
with food, drink, musical instruments, even gifts
for me: wood for the stove in the back, scrap metal
for my Gorky, drawing paper stolen from the WPA
Poster Workshop. There was a miraculous lot of
food, mostly cold things like sausages, cheeses,
gehockteh leber, potato salads, breads, bowls of
depression Jell-O, and suchlike, but Harry's sister
Golda, always one for dramatic entrances and exits,
came sweeping in out of the snowy night bearing
a huge pot of steaming hot kasha with noodles and
chicken gizzards, and O.B. and his girl brought
backbone and dumplings and a kettle of hambone
soup we warmed up on my hot plate with Leo's
beans. Oh boy, I can taste it still! Feel it, hear it
still!

*"I met a man the other day I never met
    before,
He asked me if I wanted a job ashovelin'
    iron ore.
And I asked him what the wages was, and
    he said ten cents a ton,
And I said, Aw fella, go scratch your neck
    I'd rather be on the bum!*

    *I am a bum, a jolly old bum,
    And I live like a royal Turk . . ."*

Even Simon turned up, unable to stay away,
since it was he after all who'd arranged Maxie's
trip to Spain through his Party contacts. He and
Harry managed to keep most of the crowd between
them for the half hour that Simon stayed around,
but it was good just to see them both in the same
room again. Golda thought so, too, and gave Simon
a big conspiratorial hug, though she carefully chose
a moment when her brother was distracted, pushing
Gus through another verse. Golda's only heresy
was her big heart, and no doubt they both forgave
her. As they might, in the end, forgive each other.
For all the horror of the Spanish Civil War, it
was at least doing this, reconciling decent people
like Simon and Harry. The Popular Front. I believe in the Popular Front—not in the military
sense of a force allied by fear to confront a common enemy, but in the positive sense of an avant-
garde of humankind drawn together by love and

reason (even now I can hear Leo snorting at this, though it is he who lives by it) to create a better world. Like the *hora* they used to dance down near Herzl Junior College in Independence Square. At the time, watching them in their bouncy rounds, I thought they were silly. Grown-ups acting like kindergartners—like stupid little pishers, as my late uncle would say. I was twelve years old then and going senile. Now I only regret my two left feet. In Barcelona, they say, they have a dance much like it. That night I supposed I would soon be learning it. I told Maxie so: "I'm coming, too," I said, lifting my glass, "as soon as I can." He met my foolish grin with a solemn gaze. "You're a good friend, Meyer," he said. "You're the best friend I have." I was deeply moved by this, and thought: He's saying goodbye. Suddenly I wished he wasn't going. Farewells have always been easy for me, but this one wasn't. I met Maxie a few years ago at the Jewish Training School and we became close friends as though in spite of our differences. I told him that day we met that I was making welded sculptures. He looked solemnly at his hands and said: "Well, I am making a nation." He did not speak Yiddish, but pure Hebrew, though otherwise he was impatient with books and thought the fine arts a waste of practical skills. He seemed to think a nation was something you built entirely with your hands, and if he's alive I'm sure he still

48

does. But that night, at the party, he walked over and stood in front of my mask of Gorky. He stared up at it for a long time and then he said: "I don't understand it, Meyer. I don't know why anyone would do such a thing. But when I am away from here, I know it will be the most important memory I have of you. It will come to my mind and I will think about it then." At that moment I felt certain he knew more about my work than anyone alive, but I didn't know how to put this in words, so I said nothing. I regret that, of course, and have worried since that he might have thought he'd hurt my feelings.

Around us meanwhile the party was in full swing, and I was soon swept into it again, heating up food, rinsing forks and glasses, bringing in the ice I'd been making in buckets in the backyard and chopping it up with one of my sculpting chisels, joining in the songs (*"Solidarity forever! Solidarity forever . . ."*) and hugs and conversations, the laughter and shouting. "Salud, Meyer!" "Salud, Ilya!" I felt an unbelievable intensity welling up about me, even when the chatter was about nothing more serious than chainletters and chicken factories, Charlie McCarthy or Chick Webb . . .

> ". . . *In our hands is placed a power greater than their hoarded gold;*
> *Greater than the might of armies, magnified a thousand-fold.*

49

*We can bring to birth a new world from
    the ashes of the old.
For the union makes us strong!*

>   *Solidarity forever!
    Solidarity forever . . . !"*

There was a lot of talk about Spain, of course,
about art and theater and music, writing, film,
swing bands, politics, all the things these friends
of mine were not only interested in, but working
and living with every day. I thought: These are the
most beautiful people in the world, I'm lucky just
to be able to have them around me! "You will eat,
by and by!" they sang, crowding up around the
overloaded trestle table.

"The change from a handicraft mode of production to the machine age has alienated and isolated
the artist," Simon was saying over the noise, holding up the unfinished torso of a quarterback throwing a forward pass. "Meyer is fighting this alienation with his welding, don't you see, humanizing,
as it were, the industrial product . . ."

"No shit . . ."

>   *". . . Work and pray, live on hay,
    You'll get pie in the sky when you die!"*

Simon took up a collection for the Brigade before he left, and Golda promised Maxie to keep
a steady flow of cigarettes and warm socks coming

to him in Spain, as she was already doing for Dave and the others. We drank to that. We were drinking to everything. And eating. And talking. "Hell, that guy's got the imagination of a goddamn mirror," someone said and winked at me. "Where's the mustard?"

> *"Hold, Madrid, for we are coming,*
> *I.B. men be strong . . . !"*

Father Divine was mentioned, Mother Bloor, test-tube babies and Baby Snooks. "What I'm sick of is art as a kinda jazzy framed wallpaper for rich cats!"—this was O.B., his voice intense but his soft brown face smiling serenely: "Art's gotta go public, baby!" I think we were talking about a *New Masses* article on the Ash Can School of American art, but at the same time all around us people were joking about O'Neill's Nobel and Paul Muni's Oscar ("Imagine! Our own little Muni Weisenfreund!"), endorsing Sal Hepatica ("One dose, honey, and I was relaxed as twilight!") or arguing about John L. Lewis as Working-Class Hero or capitalist lackey or next President of the United States or the driver of a Cadillac V-12, and it was all getting mixed up, deliciously mixed up. "Sure, times are better," Leo was saying, tugging on his long mustaches. "Sure, there's more money around. You used to only get forty dollars to beat up a worker a couple of years ago. Now it's sixty, and for breaking his legs a bonus and a paid vacation!"

> *"Come, Workers, sing a rebel song,*
> *A song of love and hate;*
> *Of love unto the lowly and of hatred to*
>   *the great . . ."*

By now, the wine was beginning to taste very smooth, in fact it had no taste at all, and when O.B. offered me his reefer, I took a deep puff without even coughing. "Wow, it's like *A Night at the Opera* in here!" O.B.'s girlfriend laughed, as someone bumped her up against him, and I laughed with her. Then it seemed I couldn't stop laughing. When the Black Baron wandered in and Harry asked him in a corny Baron Munchausen accent, "Vot you tink, Sharlie, all dis pipple?", I couldn't even keep my feet, but fell giggling to my knees. Thérèse, infected by my giddiness, bugged her eyes at me, gapped her mouth, and sang out: "Aw, I once was as pure as a lily, an' nobody called me no cow . . .

> *"Mah booty was sweet as a rosebud,*
> *But lookit the dam' thing now—!"*

And—*"Woops!"*—she tossed her paper skirts over her head. We were all laughing by then. "Hey! Ain't dot luffly?" "Hee hee!" I was rolling around, unable to stand, feeling wildly silly but wonderful. "Meyer, you goofy ass," Jesse laughed, baptizing me with a spray of whiskey, "you oughta git drunk more often!" It was around then, or maybe a little after, it's all a bit confused, that I danced my *kazatzke*. And it was some time after this, hours maybe, long after midnight certainly, when most of the people had left, that I found myself sitting on the concrete floor of my barnlike studio with those close friends remaining (I'd spread some dusty old canvas for everybody to sit on, or seemed to have, maybe someone else did this), huddled in our overcoats, listening to Jesse sing old folk songs, new union songs, joining in when we knew the words or thought we did:

> *"A redheaded woman took me out to dine,*
> *Says "Love me, baby, leave your union*
> *behind."*
> *Get thee behind me, Satan, travel on down*
> *the line.*
> *I am a union man, gonna leave you*
> *behind."*

Harry knew some old Yiddish songs from Poland and O.B. some country blues—I especially remember one called "The Broke and Hongry Blues"— which he claimed to have learned from some blind guy with a peg leg. I'd found a tattered stocking cap for my head, had stuffed some newspapers— Hoover blankets, we used to call them on the road— inside my shirt, I was feeling very warm and happy.

The bottles had been emptied, though I still clutched my wine bottle in one hand, licking at the neck from time to time as though to hold back sweet time. I really didn't want it to end. In my other hand, I held a little Hasidic dancer, whittled from wood, the first piece of sculpture I ever did—someone had asked to see it earlier in the evening (maybe it was this that had led to the dance, or else followed it), and I hadn't let go of it after. It was, I suddenly understood, huddled there on the floor, an image of my father, though I have no memory of him, and as far as I know he never danced, nor followed Hasidim.

Past Jesse's head on the broad south wall, my mask of Maxim Gorky, made of welded bits of scrap metal and nearly ten feet tall (all that my warehouse ceiling permitted and more than the door allows), was taking shape. The wide forehead with its peasant hairline and deep worry lines, the high cheekbones, drooping mustache: these parts, though still incomplete, could be made out now and understood. By coincidence, I'd been reading—and been much moved by—*My Universities* when Gorky died last year, and I had thrown myself impulsively into the project, thinking: This is worth a lifetime. I'd thought I was ready for it, felt sure I had the skills now, the insight, the right relationship. I hadn't reckoned, however, with the eyes. Hundreds of sketches were stuck up on the wall around the face, hundreds more had been destroyed, and I hadn't got the eyes right yet on one of them. Those wise, piercing, compassionate eyes of Maxim Gorky, who cannot see enough of life. The old wounded eyes of Alexei Maximovitch Peshkov who has seen too much. In my imaginings, I could picture the entire face down to its least detail, but could only see deep empty spaces where the eyes should be. But tonight, I thought, tonight, if I weren't so drunk, I might almost be able—

"Hey, Meyer," Leo was saying, "let's fix some coffee and build a fire in your stove."

He was right. The studio was very cold. You could see your breath. Outside, snow was tumbling past my front shop window, vertical one moment, then suddenly horizontal the next as wind gusts whipped it. We struggled to our feet, the ten or eleven of us still there, and went back to my little room behind the studio, where I ate, slept, washed, and even, especially in the winter, did most of my work. There, on my old iron bed, we found Gloomy Gus screwing Harry's sister Golda.

Golda stared up at us in terror and confusion— she's no virgin, Golda, she's been married once and has lived with a boyfriend or two since, but she is, as they say, a good Jewish girl, and this was not her style at all—but she held on to Gus all the same. Gus hadn't seemed to notice we'd come in, he just kept thumping away: white-cheeked, very hairy, and professional. His lips moved faintly as though he were timing himself.

"Vos . . . you sh— vos *tut* zich—!?" Harry choked, his voice cracking with embarrassment and rage, but too stunned for the moment to leap on Gus and drag him off. I braced myself for the worst, glanced around for things that might break.

"Don't do anything, Harry!" Golda pleaded throatily, wrapping her big soft thighs all the tighter around Gus's bucking arse. Her eyes reminded me of some of my rejected sketches for Gorky's eyes: desperate, aggrieved, soulful, but reflecting something more like irrational panic than wisdom. Over their heads was a quote I'd pinned up from Gorky's *Childhood:* "Our life is amazing not only for the vigorous scum of bestiality with which it is overgrown, but also for the bright and wholesome creative forces gleaming beneath." *"I'm in love!"* she cried.

Harry's mouth opened and shut three or four times, gasping for air like a beached fish. Harry in his poems celebrated free love and he never interfered with his sister's affairs, but he was clearly unprepared for this. He seemed to be trying to say something like "Get off!" or "Give up!," but before he could get it out, Gus suddenly arched his back, slammed powerfully into Golda, and unleashed an orgasm that made her yelp and cross her eyes.

"Hey! Hey—shit shtik!" Harry croaked, finding

his wind at last, grabbing Gus roughly by the shoulder. *"I'm telling you—!"*

Gus turned slowly, imperturbably, to gaze up at Harry from Golda's flushed and ample bosom where he'd fallen, and after a moment a flicker of recognition crossed his bearded face. He lifted himself with brisk expertise out of Golda, stood with a jerky little hop, pulled on his shorts and trousers, tucked in his shirt, buckled his belt, cleared his throat and, standing there more or less at attention, sang "The Internationale" straight through, not missing a word: "Arise, ye prisoners of starvation! Arise, ye wretched of the earth . . . !"

We all dropped back in amazement, foolish grins twitching at the corners of our mouths (O.B. was laughing openly, his white teeth gleaming against his black face, and his girl was giggling helplessly, her face ducked against O.B.'s chest; later, I accomplished a wire-and-plaster study for a sculpture of the two of them like that, calling it, and meaning no irony at all, "After Guadalajara"), all except Harry and Golda—Golda lay tearful and naked on my bed like a pinned moth, breaking out all over her body in a pink mottled rash ("How many on our flesh have fattened . . . ?" Gus was singing), while Harry stood rooted to the floor and white with shock. He didn't even move when Gus finished his recital (*"The Internationale shall be the human race!"*), raised two clenched fists in a

V, smiled as though accepting applause, and strode out. We had to shake poor Harry and smack his cheeks before he snapped out of it. Golda had by then roused herself, grabbed up her clothes and, rolling her eyes toward the ceiling, fled the room, possibly to chase after Gus, maybe just to escape her brother's wrath. Harry wasn't angry, though. He just shook his head stupidly like an old man and muttered: "That f'kucken Karl Marx! That f'kucken Karl Marx . . ."

Just how Gus managed that seduction, I eventually witnessed for myself and at Golda's request. Poor Golda. Ordinarily buoyant, chatterboxy, rather plain and unmade-up and simple as water, a happy, open woman with a good heart and a fair amount of worldly wisdom, she suddenly became estranged and melancholic, more beautiful in a soft and vulnerable way, but more ludicrous too, puppy-eyed and dolled up like a schoolgirl: a poor hapless maiden, we all supposed, suffering from unrequited love. Except when he was copulating with her, which was about once a week, off and on—or I should say, on and off—Gus didn't know she existed. The old story, you might say—but no, he *really* didn't know she existed. She had to throw herself in his path. If on these rare occasions he had rejected her, even insulted or abused her, she might in time have got over him—she's no child, after all, and ordinarily has a good sense of humor. But each time it was apparently exactly the same thing all over again—a textbook seduction, stunning orgasm, then briskly out and gone without so much as a wink or a fare-thee-well, leaving Golda spread out, flushed, gasping, and ever deeper and deeper in love. I'd see her often, lurking about my studio, a forlorn and dark-eyed creature utterly unlike the Golda I once knew, hoping only to catch a glimpse of her lover, but disappearing the moment Harry or one of the others turned up. She did catch him there a time or two, and discreetly I left them to it.

But one day she came up to me and, tears running down her soft cheeks, she said: "Meyer, you got to help me! Am I crazy or what?"

"Sure, Golda, you're crazy," I said. I was up on a ladder, working on Gorky's forehead. It occurred to me that Gorky had not said much that was useful on the subject of sexual love, but in this I felt yet another bond with him. I did not know or care much about it either, especially that of other people. "All people in love are crazy."

She didn't seem to hear me. She was staring at, or rather through, a little row of flowers made out of brass hinges, screws, and the like, one of a group of things I'd been working on since Maxie's party. My Jarama flowers, I called them. "Meyer, listen, it's always the same, exactly the same . . ."

I thought at first she meant that all her affairs had come to nothing in the end, which was mostly true, and I started to make something up about the flowers she was staring past (maybe, also, I wanted her to notice them), but then it came to me that she might be trying to say something else. "What's exactly the same, Golda?"

"What he says. What he does. The whole shmeer. Every word, every look, every touch, just the same. It's like going to a movie you seen before. Except you end up getting . . . having . . ." She sighed, looked up at me. Yes, she's in trouble, I thought, I could see it. "Is that you up there, Meyer? Maybe this is all just a bad dream, hunh?"

"No, it's me, Golda," I said, crawling down off the ladder, pulling off my welding goggles: "See?" I shut down the acetylene and oxygen, released the screw on the pressure regulators, drained the lines. In my mind's eye I still saw that deep furrow over Gorky's eye I was working on. The truth is beyond all commiseration . . . "C'mon, let's have some coffee, you can tell me about it."

She seemed to calm down and become the old Golda once more, but when we reached the back and she saw my cot, she got all shaky and tearful again. I kept quiet, letting her find her own time and way to get it off her chest. I didn't exactly want to know about it, but I knew she'd tell me regardless. Gorky has a line in his *Childhood:* "I might liken myself as a child to a beehive to which various common ordinary people brought the honey of their knowledge and views of life. . . . Often the honey was dirty and bitter, but being knowledge, it was honey, nonetheless." People have always come to me like that, too. I rarely ask any questions, but they tell me things anyway. "It starts," she said, "with the way he looks up at me, how he suddenly recognizes me, the way the lid on one eye droops a bit and his lips come apart, how he tilts his head like he's thinking about something very serious, and then how he smiles, so warm, so good, a little movement he makes with his hand, like a touch across the space between us, and I feel a tingle. 'Golda!' he says. Such a nice deep voice he has, Meyer, throaty and solemn like a rabbi. 'Golda, I been looking for you!' And then he takes my hand . . ."

She described it all, phrase by phrase, gesture by gesture, touch by touch—I found myself getting excited in spite of myself—and exactly what happened to her each step of the way. "There's no grabbing, no fumbling, his hands slide from my face to inside my underwear like magic, Meyer, like water running over pebbles in a brook, you know? Gemitlech-like, going from some place to another place, sure, but remembered like being everywhere at once, and he is whispering in my ear and kissing the insides of my legs and smiling down at me from above, and I don't know where I am anymore! 'Surrender to the ancient force inside you, Golda,' he says, 'struggle against death!' Is he

62

kidding? The surrender is over, he's—*zetz!*—inside me already, he's—*ah!*—my clothes are gone but—*oi!*—filling me . . . !" The last part got rather blurred, but by then the words weren't very important anyway.

She lay on my cot after, her clothes sweaty and rumpled, her hand between her thighs, her face suddenly aged and filled with so much sorrow I lost all my own excitement and wished only to hold her like a child and give her comfort. "Meyer," she whispered, "would you do me a favor?"

"Sure, Golda . . ."

"Watch him, Meyer. Watch what he does to me."

"You mean while he—? Well, I don't know, Golda, I don't much like—"

"Please, Meyer. For me. He'll come here tomorrow. Keep the others away and watch. Tell me what happens, the whole megillah, tell me if I'm crazy or what."

As usual, spineless as ever, I could not say no. The next day was Friday and Gus turned up as expected. I'd chased the others off, telling them my aunt was coming to visit. (And what would have happened, I was to wonder later on, when it was all clear to me, if Gus had taken my crazy aunt on?) I didn't even have time to hide, but Gus didn't seem to register my presence, and Golda after the first minute or two was conscious of nothing except Gus. And it was all true, the whole transaction, word for word, move by move. Gus entered the studio, walked to the back to get fed, noticing nothing en route, and there she was. She looked frightened and painfully self-conscious, yet approachable as a park bench; he seemed as insentient as ever, staring at her like she was the horizon. But then suddenly there was that flicker of recognition, the little gestures, and Golda, like Pavlov's dog, began to respond. "Golda!" he said gently. "Golda, I've been looking for you!" He took her hand.

It was very smooth, very professional, yet sincere and intense at the same time. He went through the entire routine, just as Golda had recounted it, but though I'd heard it all before and stood objectively apart, trying vainly to apply Freud to what I saw, it was such an absorbing spectacle it all seemed like new. I tried to watch his hands, but I, too, got caught up in the timelessness of his performance and could not remember afterwards exactly how he undressed her. "Oh, Dick!" she groaned (she was the only one of us who ever used his real name). "Take me! Love me! Save me!" I left before the climax (he was technologically up-to-date, I'd noticed, using one of those slide fasteners on his fly instead of buttons), having seen that part before, went outside and planted some flowers in the vacant lot next to my studio, thinking: It is true that love is a momentary denial of reality and death—but then, is that its true and secret function: to serve as a defense mechanism against other forms of madness? I realized I was very agitated and falling back on defense mechanisms of my own.

After Gus had fed himself on my food and left, I went back in and found Golda sitting on my cot, dazed, a bit desolate, but not unhappy. She was dressed but not tucked in, and held in her hands, which were shaking slightly, what I thought at first was a handkerchief, but what I then recognized as her underpants. She looked soft, fat, somnolent, but, as always after one of these episodes, years younger than her age. "Well, Meyer?" she whispered. "Am I crazy? Did you see?"

"I saw, Golda. It's like you said. The whole thing. It's very strange . . . every time, just like that?"

She smiled wearily, stood and pulled her underwear on. "Sometimes he doesn't call me Golda," she said sadly, gazing off through the walls of my studio. She smoothed her skirt down, tucked her blouse in; it was the kind of costume little girls wore to the country on weekend outings, though it was still winter in Chicago.

But then a few days later she staggered into my studio all bruised up, her eyes blackened, a tooth missing in front and her jaw swollen. As soon as she saw me, she started to cry. I scrambled down the ladder. I thought she might have been hit by a car.

"It was Dick," she wailed stiffly through her swollen jaw. "He hit me . . . !"

"My God, Golda!"

She fell forward on my shoulder and I started to embrace her, but she winced and pulled back: "Oh! I hurt all over!" she bawled.

I led her gently to the back, turned on the hot plate to heat up coffee. "How . . . how did it happen, Golda?" I asked. I was very upset and nearly tipped over the coffeepot, while setting it on the burner.

"He tried to kill me! He stole my purse!"

"Why? Why did he do such a thing?"

"I don't know, I don't know what's happened!" she sobbed. "Oh, God help me, Meyer, I think he's ruptured something inside me!"

"But did you say something? Did you do anything to make him—?"

She wiped her eyes on her sleeve and looked up at me. There was such a depth of sadness in her eyes, such a terrible mix of despair and longing, that I thought I was going to cry myself to see them. I'd put a box of cookies on the table, and absently she picked one up and bit into it—she gave a little yelp of pain and clutched her mouth as though trying to keep the teeth that remained from falling out. "All I did," she mumbled through her fingers, "was ask him why it was always the same."

"And just for that he—?"

"I went to see him at the theater. He starts up when he sees me, just like always. I stop him. I says, 'Tell me what you really think of me, Dick. I'm not a child,' I says, 'you don't have to lie to me, I'm nearly twenty-nine'—forgive me, Meyer, I just couldn't . . ."

"But you think that's why he hit you? Just because you lied about your age—?"

"I don't know, I don't know. All I'm sure is the minute I said 'twenty-nine,' something very peculiar come over him. Suddenly, he stops staring at me like he's Valentino and starts looking more like Wolfman—Meyer, I can't tell you, it was awful! Geferlech! He ducks his head between his shoulders and he squats down like he's got cramps or something, holding himself up with one hand, but balling the other one up like he's gonna hit somebody. . . ."

"Oh no!" I remembered that night I'd met him, the whirr-*click!* as I'd switched cues on him; we'd tested him a few times since and it was always the same. "So that's what . . . !"

"Yes, he's snarling and grunting and showing his teeth like some kinda mad dog or something, quivering all over. I was scared. He rears his tokus

67

up. I says, 'Wait a minute, Dick, we can talk about this—' And—*plats!*—he hits me! He just bucks forward, smacks into my belly and klops me clean through a wall in the set, off the stage, and into the orchestra!"

"My God, Golda!"

"My purse flies outa my hands. He grabs it in midair, hides it in his elbow, hunches his head down and shlepps it right outa the theater! Oh, Meyer! *I just wanna die!*"

I looked into her eyes. The flesh around them was puffy and discolored, but that would go away. She's seen a lot, I thought. Maybe almost enough. "Golda, would you model for me?"

She pulled back in surprise, as though to ask: You, too, Meyer? I realized it wasn't the right time to have asked her. "Meyer, you know I can't . . . I don't do that sort of thing . . ."

"No, I mean just your eyes, I want to try to do your eyes."

She stared at me a moment, her face still taut and damp with tears. Then she relaxed, took a sip of the coffee, wincing a bit, and smiled gently with cracked, swollen lips. "You're a funny boy, Meyer," she said.

On my way to Polly's Fishmarket on North Avenue, I pass a movie theater with a poster advertising a Coming Attraction: *The Last Train from Madrid*, starring Dorothy Lamour. "A hair-raising experience," it says. "*The first motion picture based on the Spanish War* . . . Takes no sides." Instant entertainment from the world's atrocities. "WAR IS SWELL . . . when a hero can succeed in winning the love of a lady like Dorothy Lamour, says Gilbert Roland." So much for heroism, for the struggle against oppression and injustice, laying down one's life for his fellow men. Of course, not so instant: given the lag time in motion-picture production, "quick-thinking, fast-acting Paramount Pictures" must have started shooting before Franco did. And as for entertainment, who am I to cast stones? My Jarama flowers, fallen warriors, poised athletes, even my Gorky mask: how much is really a gift to the world, how much a premeditated theft of its substance?

"Hey, whadda udder fella look like, Mayor?" Polly asks with an appreciative whistle.

"I hit a door, Polly."

"Sure, sure, lucky da door don' shoot you! I hope she wort' it! Hey, you should see da mullets, Mayor, you wooden believe!"

"Not today, Polly. Just a bit of mackerel, please. And a couple fishheads for my cat, if you have any."

"Sure, I got fishhead," he says, dipping into the sink. He slaps one on the drainboard, flops a red mullet out between us. "Jus' looka dat, Mayor! Ain' he gorgiss?"

"It looks delicious, Polly. Maybe tomorrow."

"Tomorra Friday, wop fishday, all gone. Nowza time, Mayor! Firs' udda munt', you got money inna pocket! Enjoy!"

The fishhead has somehow slithered back into the sink. "Well, okay. But a smaller one." He doesn't hear my qualification, starts wrapping up the mullet he's shown me. "For you, chip," he assures me. Oh well. For the Baron's sake, I rationalize, reaching for the bill crumpled up under the railroad spikes in my pocket. Polly dips for another generous handful of heads and other slippery debris. Jesse won't mind. We'll share it with Harry and Ilya if they come along. My friends often let me do their fish-buying for them so I can establish credit for the Baron. For all of us actually: the

70

Baron's often had to share his windfalls with the rest of us during hard times in the form of stew or, when Golda lends a hand, fishcakes.

"You wan' some ice crim, Mayor? My sister make."

"Next time, Polly," I say firmly, snatching up the parcels before the fish can slip into the sink again.

He shrugs, surrenders the change. "Take care da eye, Mayor—an' stay way marrit leddies! Drive you wreck an' ruin!"

This was more or less that Hearst reporter's theory about "whatever happened" to Gloomy Gus: a great athlete unmanned by a fatal weakness for women. The Samson syndrome. "That sumbitch couldn't get enough, M'ar," he told me, sitting back against my cold stove, his voice soft with awe and envy. He was staring at my iron bed (we'd just exchanged a few anecdotes, mentioning no names), shaking his head. "He was a goddamn legend. His dingdong was like the community relay baton, he poked it in every pussy in this fuckin' country, from kid movie stars to the President's grandmaw, he hardly had time for anything else. Finally, the way I figure it, all that humpin' just shook his marbles loose." There was a grain of truth in this. Or perhaps I should say, a seed of truth. The full title of that song about him was "You Gotta Be a Football Hero, To Get Along with the Beautiful

Girls," and sometimes that did seem to be the point of it. His sexual exploits were truly notorious, as famous as his touchdowns, really, and he's still the subject of a lot of jokes—only Friday I heard one down at Sam's Place near the Republic Steel mills, the one about Gloomy Gus losing a bet that he could screw all forty-six of the Radio City Rockettes in one night, giving up in defeat finally at forty-three ("Twenty-nine, more like," Leo interrupted with a wink at me) with the apology that he couldn't understand what was wrong, the rehearsal that afternoon had gone just fine. But that joke had more truth in it than the Hearst reporter's theory, even down to the sterile mechanized sex of the Rockettes. For it wasn't really dissipation that brought down Gloomy Gus. Simon maybe was closer to it with what he calls "the inherent contradictions of the American dream," though it seems likely to me any dream of order would do.

Telling jokes in Sam's Place was the quiet part about Friday. Mostly it was hard work and finally not a little dangerous, my own most obvious souvenir of the day being my tenderized eye. I'd like to say the eye was a consequence of the sterile mechanized anality of the Chicago police force, their familiar and libidinous choreography of swinging saps and truncheons, but it wasn't as simple as that. Leo had personally asked me to come down: the place was full of strangers, one of the

drawbacks of the movement's new fluidity and national solidarity, and Leo was sure several of them
were company spies. "Now that I've lost Jesse,
Meyer, I need someone near me I can trust." It was
Friday, the day I always relinquished my studio to
Golda and Gus, so I needed some place to go anyway. I've never been that far south in Chicago
before—nearly 120 blocks below the Loop—and I
was surprised at how much open space there was.
Even the steel plant is built low to the ground down
there, sprawling about loosely to the south over
some three hundred gritty acres between the Calu-
met River and the Pennsy Railroad tracks. The
CIO organizers had set up their headquarters in a
friendly working-class tavern called Sam's Place,
situated at the northeast edge of a grassy field looking across at the front gates of the Republic mill.
In fact there's a well-worn beeline path diagonally
across the field from the gates to Sam's Place, no
doubt laid there by Sam's regulars. No beer at
Sam's Friday, though, only water. There were a
few ice-cream and soft-drink vendors around, a lot
of picnic food, and some did have their own bottles, but there wasn't all that much drinking going
on. A policy of the union organizers, of course, but
it was anyway too hot for alcohol. Hot and sunny.
The field between us and the plant seemed almost
to glow in the blazing light, and I thought at the
time: It's a stage, waiting there for us, almost

magical in its alluring power. For the present we
are all hovering in the wings, but who on either
side will be able to resist its shimmering pull?

There were many that seemed unable to resist it
that afternoon, and Leo was worried about them.
He and the rest of the organizers tried to distract
them with softball games, pamphleteering, speeches,
safety and marching drills, first-aid training, idle
legwork, but it was very hot and people were impatient. A lot of them distrusted the organizers,
resented being manipulated in any way. Others
thought the organizers were moving too slowly for
reasons they couldn't understand. They wanted to
get this over with and get back to work. Why wait
for Girdler to bring in reinforcements? This waiting was no good. Only action would change anything. Why not at least march across to the plant,
get close enough to reach the men still inside with
loudspeakers, shame the honest ones into coming
out? Not even the organizing committee was in
complete agreement about strategy, torn between
the reluctant voices and the rash. But a Memorial
Day picnic had been called for Sunday when other
workers and their families could turn up, a wooden
stage was being built, folksingers and speakers had
been scheduled, Gloomy Gus included, there was a
newsreel guy expected from Paramount Pictures;
it made no sense to rush things, not to Leo anyway,

so he used me most of the day scouting out hotheads and helping him cool them down.

It was a long day. The heat and the glare didn't
help, the sweat, the short tempers. It was like those
long July days out in San Francisco three years
ago during the dock strike, only grittier. Leo
noticed it, too. They'd brought out the National
Guard in San Francisco with machineguns and
rifles, and Leo worried about it happening here. It
made him feel tempted to side with the hotheads,
go now and get the jump on them. He hated all
those scabs in there, knew a lot of them were ruth-
less armed hoods, could even see the propaganda
value in provoking them. And he was upset about
his UAW friends Frankensteen and Reuther, who'd
been badly beaten Wednesday up in Dearborn by
a goon squad hired by Ford. Plainclothes cops, it
was rumored: someone saw a badge, or handcuffs.
"Where is Richie," Leo had remarked wryly, "now
that we need him?" He was referring to San Francisco again, 1934. After a dozen good men had
been shot out there on Bloody Thursday, Blaine
had caught a scab trying to sneak off the company
ship for a rendezvous with his girlfriend, had made
some buddies hold the scab's legs across a curb,
and had jumped up and down on them. Richie is
now a commissar with the Lincolns in Spain, we've
heard. And that was another thing. The dusty field

between us and the mills with its scraggly marsh grass and stunted shrubs looked too much like the pictures we'd seen of the country around Madrid. It looked like a place where people went to die. About a week after the bombing of Guernica, I'd got it in my head that Maxie had been killed. It was stupid, I had no reason for it, he probably wasn't even in Spain yet. And I distrust all premonitions, hate such rubbish as precognition and mental telepathy (one of my aunt's more appalling quirks: needless to say, she went running to the old folks' home screaming that my uncle was dead about ten times before he finally kicked off—and that day she was happily playing bridge with her North Lawndale cronies). In my case (as in hers), a projection of guilt, I supposed. But still I couldn't shake off the feeling that Maxie was dead. And it was with me like some kind of morbid affliction all day Friday.

Toward sundown, the sky behind the plant reddening like a taunt, Leo got a report from a guy named Bill, who'd also been helping him ("He's okay, he's got good calluses," Leo explained), that there was a group planning to march on the plant as soon as it got dark. Bill estimated there were about a hundred of them, but that they'd take others with them. He said he'd tried to talk them out of it, as Leo had asked, but they'd got pretty hostile toward him, accusing him of being a lackey and a company fink. A lot of the local workers had drifted away around suppertime, the women and children as well, the crowd was becoming increasingly hard-core, many of them from out of town, and, as Bill pointed out, there was now a lot more drinking going on. This was true, I'd noticed it myself. Several members of the organizing committee had left by now as well, and I could see that Leo was seriously considering joining the exodus. He argued with individuals that a march on the plant now would serve no purpose at all, that it would only give the police an opportunity to beat up and arrest a lot of men we would need on Sunday, and that it might even give the authorities an excuse to bring in enough force to make the Memorial Day demonstration impossible. As individuals, they all tended to agree with him, but as a group they still seemed determined to march. They wanted something to happen, they didn't care what. "Ah well, it'll give us something to talk about on Sunday, I guess," he said finally, turning to a guy with a bottle. "Lemme have a swig of the people's cornjuice, Smitty." He took a deep suck on the bottle, handed it to me with an airy wheeze. "Have a bracer, Meyer," he said with a crooked smile, barely visible now in the deepening dusk, "and get ready for history."

By the time we'd formed up outside Sam's Place, there were nearly a thousand of us, and Leo, ever the pragmatist, had not only by now accepted the inevitable, he was even helping to organize it. Instead of marching straight across the rough field where we might stumble and fall in the dark, we headed south down Green Bay Avenue, keeping the field on our right. There was still a faint glow on it, as if the bright day had left a residue, as in phosphorescent rock. It looked mysterious, almost otherworldly. Leo had put me on the right flank, near the guy named Smitty, whom we'd both come to suspect of being a police plant and agitator (maybe it was the lethal quality of his booze that had given him away), and told me to keep an eye on him while he took the other flank. At 117th Street, we turned west toward the main gate, but we didn't get far: the police were waiting for us there. It was as though they'd known all along we were coming. Of course we'd been shouting a lot in the dark echoey night, and a couple of cops had got pushed aside further up the street, it was hardly a secret. But even before we'd reached them, they seemed to be in our midst. That was when I got my black eye, and a bruise or two elsewhere besides. It was pitch-dark and there was a lot of confusion, fists and clubs flying, bricks as well, but I had no doubt who it was who hit me. I'm used to looking at the world through dark goggles, after all, and seeing more than most. I'd been knocked to the ground and was having a hard time getting up. I heard shots being fired, people screaming. It was Bill and Smitty who rescued me, dragging me away from the melee, upfield toward Sam's Place. The strikers were quickly routed by their own confusion, but a lot of heads got broken first. Some would need a hospital. The vanguard especially took a beating, but Leo, as I knew he'd be, was all right. "Sorry, Meyer," he said when he saw me, and as far as I could tell, he truly was.

"Bill," I said.

"That sonuvabitch . . ."

"Bill and Smitty." They'd disappeared, of course, ostensibly to hurl themselves back into the fight, but it was clear they'd used me as the means to their own withdrawal. I'd seen them push the men in front off balance and into the police, then, yelling curses all the while at the cops (these were ritual phrases, repeated woodenly like recognition signals), start laying about wildly, as though fighting off unseen monsters. And it was Bill who, glancing over his shoulder to take aim, had laid me out with his elbow. If it was his elbow. Felt harder than one. It might have been about then, sprawling in the dirt and getting kicked and stepped upon in the night-dark turmoil, that I began to feel I might be able to live with myself if I didn't after all make it to Spain. Amazingly, some of these guys do this sort of thing every Saturday night just for fun; I prefer a little music on the radio and a handful of soft clay.

The next day Leo let a rumor start circulating that the committee had identified at least five company spies in their midst, and that they would be "dealt with" by all the comrades after sundown. "Bill" and "Smitty" (we no longer supposed those were their real names) were occasionally mentioned. They kept up a good front through the afternoon, but by sundown they had cleared out. Along with seventeen others. "Thanks, Meyer," Leo said, and sent me home.

It's still chilly and overcast, but the rain's stopped by the time I reach my street in Old Town. In the school playground a block or so before my studio, boys are playing a ballgame. Other times of the year, it would be football or basketball, today it's baseball: the Cubs versus the White Sox, about five to a side, they're taking names like Billy Herman and Luke Appling, Dixie Walker, Jimmy Collins. Both teams—the real ones—are having good seasons, fighting right now for second place in their respective leagues, so the boys have a lot of pride in being who they are. The kid pitching for the White Sox five is, not surprisingly, calling himself Bill Dietrich, that down-and-outer the Sox picked up earlier this year on waivers who astonished everyone this week with his unlikely no-hitter. The kid even wears glasses like Dietrich, maybe that's why they've let him pitch.

I remember those games. I was never good enough to be Cobb or Wagner, I was always content to be somebody like Frank Schulte or Three-Finger

Brown. For me, it wasn't whether you won or lost, but it wasn't exactly how you played the game either. The other boys used to complain I wasn't trying my best—I was, but what was best for me wasn't the same thing as it was for them. Participation was what I loved about ballgames, still do. Participation in the movement. It's what I love about socialism, theater, life itself. Even sculpture in a slightly different way: all the movement then is between me and my figures, but it's a real involvement just the same, a real dialectic. Probably I have Levite blood in me from somewhere, more in love with the choreography of gesture than with its aims. Sometimes this was useful in a ballgame, often it was not. As in life. Gliding toward a flyball, I often arrived too late for the catch; swinging easily around the bases, I'd run into easy putouts. This didn't bother me, but it bothered the others. They said I didn't have enough "hustle."

Just the opposite from Gloomy Gus. Winning was everything for him. Or at least scoring. In a magazine interview, he once said: "I have never had much sympathy for the point of view 'It isn't whether you win or lose, but how you play the game.' One must put top consideration on the will, the desire, and the determination to win!" Ghostwriters maybe, but the sentiment—or something very close to it—was his: "I never in my life wanted to be left behind." He once had a football coach back at Whittier College, a fierce half-breed Indian ironically confined to a Quaker college and a team called the Poets, who drilled it into him every day: "You must never be satisfied with losing. You must get angry, terribly angry, about losing." Such maxims either blew right by him or else they shot straight to his center, riveting in, becoming part of the very nuts and bolts of his oddly indurate and at the same time transparent mechanism. He was a walking parody of Marx's definition of consciousness, a cartoon image of the Social Product, probably the only man in recent history with what could be called a naked superego.

"If he's a bit demented," Simon liked to say in his uninspired way, "well, he's only a mirror image of the insane nation that created him," but though there was a germ of truth in that, it was a simpleminded truth. Just like Marx's famous dictum: an overstatement in the heat of historical debate against ossified orthodoxies. Sure, we're all crazy, and society often as not—as the lowest common denominator of our collective craziness—reinforces our silliest quirks, but between our cells and the informing universe (the dimensions are awesome, and not only in space) there's a lot of action. Words, like pebbles in a brook, create eddies and murmurings, but they're not the stream itself. Dogmatic epigrams like Simon's just dam up the brook and send it flowing elsewhere.

He came up with a much more interesting remark, quite spontaneously, that night Gus tackled
my stove. While cleaning up the debris and putting
the stove back together again (we'd got Gus back
to playacting again, easing him gradually away
from the heat and excitement of football by having
him perform from a play he'd apparently written
himself called *The Little Accident*, in which he'd
played the part of a football player at Whittier
College), I related what I knew by then about his
past, the football, the girls, his timetables, the early
decisions, and I tossed out a thought that had come
to me earlier: "What if that's what we mean by
'growing up'? I mean, coming to a decision, suddenly or slowly, consciously or unconsciously, to
step out of the explosion at large and accept some
kind of structure you can work in, some arbi-
trary configuration—your own invention or bor-
rowed from others—that allows you to reduce time
to something merely functional: a material you
can cut up and construct memories with . . ."

"You mean, what if 'growing up' and 'going
nuts' are the same thing?" Leo asked.

"Well, if they are," Simon said, "then—as of
right now—they aren't anymore."

This, coming from Simon, so surprised us that
we all applauded. Gus assumed, of course, that we
were clapping for him—didn't all the world?—
and he lifted both fists above his head and flashed

a frozen smile. We got into a heated argument after that about Leo's desire to use Gus in the coming confrontation in South Chicago, Jesse and I arguing against the cynical manipulation of idiots as a form of exploitation and ultimately dangerous to the cause (what if one of them took over?), Leo, O.B., and Simon arguing variously for the impossibility of any action without "manipulation," the sheer entertainment value of the thing (this was O.B., who has walked so long at the edge of some brink or other that he's forgotten to care anymore whether he drops off or not—though reviewed as "cries of protest," his novels are really about suicide and how to enjoy it), and the paradox that in any revolution those rebelling against the society have been warped by it.

"And anyway," Leo said, "I don't think anybody's going to get hurt. Now that U.S. Steel has seen the light, these little assholes like Girdler will have to cave in, too. But we've got to stand firm, and we can use Gus here as a kind of symbol. You know, HOLD THAT LINE!"

Gus, startled, leaped to his feet, dropped into a crouch, commenced to growl. "Whoa, boy!" Jesse cried. *"Time out!"*

"Man, I'm all for you takin' this geek down there with you," O.B. laughed, "but if you do, I'm gonna come and holler '29!' "

"**H**ey, Meyer!" It's one of the boys. "I was safe, wasn't I?"

I've been watching their game in the schoolyard without thinking about it. Now I let what I've just seen pass again in slow motion before my inner eye (the one I do all my sculpting with—everything goes in there, but not everything stays, and reason has nothing to do with it; it's a lot like Gus's gearbox, now that I think about it): Bernie, the boy who asked me the question, has tried to stretch a single to a double. The kid on second was thrown the ball in plenty of time and was standing well in front of the detached chunk of sidewalk they're using for the base, but he was scared and had his eyes shut. Bernie, eyes all lit up with the joy of it (memory is the greatest illusionist of them all, I think, giving us time with one hand and taking it away with the other), bashed into him, sending the kid sprawling. Right now, he's trying very hard not to cry. "You were out, Bernie."

"See? See?" cries the other kid loudly, too

loudly, the tears springing to the corners of his eyes, reinforcing his indignation and self-righteousness. "You're out, I told ya!"

"Aw, Meyer, you're blind! He wasn't even looking what he was doing!"

"I know. He didn't tag you, you tagged the ball. If you'd been smart, instead of trying to knock him down like that, you would've just tiptoed around behind him."

Everybody laughs at that, even the kid who's been hit. "Hey, Meyer," says another, the fat boy who's playing Big Zeke Bonura over on first, "come and umpire, will ya?"

"Yeah, Meyer!"

"Can't, fellas. I've got to get on home, get some work done. Besides, I'm soaking wet, and I've got some raw fish here I have to put in the icebox."

"Aw, Meyer, just half a hour!" pleads the bespectacled White Sox pitcher.

"No, you see, a friend of mine died today, I couldn't really keep my mind on the ballgame. But, hey, that was some game you pitched Monday! You made the Hall of Fame!" The boys laugh at that, a little self-consciously maybe, but they know I'm good at pretending with them. I see Old Man Donaldson coming around the corner with his fruit cart. "I tell you what I will do, though—I'll buy you all an apple!"

They cheer at that and swarm around Donaldson's wagon to pick out the ones with the least bruises. Bernie, to get even, takes a banana, which is expensive. Donaldson is a surly old wretch and might have taken a cut at them with his horsewhip, but just then his old nag drops a load of manure, and he gets distracted picking it up, shoveling it into a bucket he keeps hanging from the side of the cart for the purpose. "Never throw nothin' away," he always says, and does so now. Bernie's slide into second base with all its inner contradictions is still playing before my inner eye, and an idea comes to me suddenly for a little football piece, something to mark Gus's performance down at Republic Steel. Not exactly what Leo had in mind maybe (I'm thinking of the lurch into freedom through all those grabbing and flailing restraints of the line, form emerging from chaotic matter), but it's the first idea of any kind I've had in a month, I have to get home and sketch it out. I pay for the apples and the banana and buy myself a box of strawberries, thinking: I'm a rich man, I can eat like the Duke of Windsor and spend all my days modeling little football and baseball players out of mud and nails—and if Leo and the others cannot see what I'm doing, then that just shows that, as with Gloomy Gus, their lives are too narrow and segmented.

"How, after all you've been through, Meyer,"

Leo once asked me, "can you fuck around making these goddamn emptyheaded palookas?"

"It's social realism," Simon said, defending me, and Leo laughed, thinking Simon was making a joke. But Simon's too dense for humor; I supposed he was thinking of all those muscular Soviet posters (though in that respect, the Fascists are even better social realists than the Soviets). Either way, he was wrong about it. True, I believe in social realism, after a fashion, but I don't think you can know it before you start. True dialectic means letting your own work teach you as you go along. Art as process, as Dewey says, as interaction, shared celebration. You have to expose yourself before the world will show itself to you: a truth from the Torah.

I often get criticized by my friends for the athletes I make (and Leo's right in a way: my welding techniques often use suggestion more than solid matter, so the heads are often, quite literally, empty). They argue that professional American sports reflect the sickness of American society: the exploitation of players, manipulation of followers, the brutality and competitiveness of the game, the record-keeping mania and personality cults, even the hokum reenactment and reinforcement of the rags-to-riches mythology. Bigtime football especially enrages them. They hate the raw, naked aggression,

the implicit imperialism in the battle for yard-
age, the dehumanizing uniforms and training schedules, the lionization of the bully, and the celebration
of violence as a way of discovering the self.

"It stinks!" Harry has barked, getting emotional.
"A shandeh, Meyer! A game of Fascists!"

"Or feudalists," I once offered in reply. "King
Quarterback and his knights in the backfield getting
all the glory, the peasant serfs up on the line taking
all the punishment . . ."

"Right! F'kucken Cossacks!"

"No wonder the game's full of goddamn Irish
Catholics," Leo said. "Either they're employed as
cops beating up working stiffs, fighting for the Fascists in Spain, stealing us blind down at City Hall,
or playing football for fucking Notre Dame!" We've
all been down on Irish Catholics of late, though one
of our best friends is—or was—a socialist priest
named Clanahan who used to live and drink over
on Larrabee; we haven't seen him since the war
broke out in Spain: had he been horrified by the
Republican massacre of priests and nuns and re-
turned to the fold, or has he, as rumored, joined
the Basque Resistance in Bilbao? (Now collapsing
under the weight of the Fascists' superior arms, sad
to say, yet another piece of today's dismaying news
mosaic.) Leo himself might once have been a Cath-
olic for all we know, depending on whether his real
name is Leopold, Leonardo, León, Leonid, or Le-

onides, all of which—and more—I've known him to use at one time or another.

"Shit, the silly ball don't even bounce straight!" Jesse put in. "It's a insult to common sense!"

"Good point!" Leo laughed. "Bunch of damn perverts!"

"F'kucken nihilists!"

Oddly, nobody ever complains about the jugglers and dancers, which belong to the same set of images: bodies in motion, for me the central thing about life. I don't miss the dead gods and vanished mysteries; motion is all the magic I need. And these figures of mine are real sentient bodies at full stretch—I don't like amoebic or inanimate shapes, I like something that knows itself and tests itself. The first print I ever owned was one of Remington's "Western Types." Remington is popular now for the wrong reasons. I'm not interested in "the American scene," the current "quest for a usable past," local color, what Harry calls "all that acreage on canvas, poor art for poor people." What excited me about Remington—and still does—is the way everything in his paintings, even the landscapes, expresses a kind of contained dynamic, some inner—perhaps tragic—force struggling, through matter, to free itself. I like things that move from the inside out, not things you look at from the outside in. I'm no voyeur, I hate the Impressionists, and was sorry when Picasso turned to Cubism, which is a hall-of-mirrors trick, not revelation—he could learn something right now from guys like Hopper and Benton. Expression is everything for me, and working as I do for the most part with figures only about a foot high, I feel that athletes, less likely to rigidify into archetypal positions than, say, workers or warriors, leave me more room to swing.

Also there's the ball. Boxers, pole-vaulters, and swimmers also work at full stretch, but I'm less drawn to them. The strange ambiguity of the ball fascinates me, so much so that it never appears in my sculptures. It often seems to be there, but it isn't. This creates a strange tension, especially with the jugglers, where the longing, the anticipation, seem more intense. Yet the jugglers always turn out too flat somehow, too static. I prefer the greater dynamism of the ballplayers, the outflung limbs, the twisted torsos, the seeming defiance of gravity and the collision of forces: they all seem actually to move, because without the logic of motion they make no sense. And football is not about violence or atavistic impulses, like Harry says, it's about balance. The line of scrimmage is a fulcrum, not a frontier, the important elements of football being speed and weight. The struggle is not for property, it's for a sudden burst of freedom. And the beauty of that. In football, as in politics, the goal, ultimately, is not ethical but aesthetic.

Of course, I admit, most footballers are probably ignorant of all this. All but the odd exception go banging unreflectively through football and then life, vaguely nostalgic at the end for something beautiful they had and lost, but unable when called upon at their testimonial dinners to put their fingers on it. This is true of all of us. One of the main tasks of socialism has to be to give all men what artists take for granted: time and incentive for reflection. Capitalism has made us overvalue action as power (the early bird gets—and consumes—the worm, and that's the beginning and end of it: a plate of worms), and contemplation has become, not merely a kind of unpatriotic idleness, but socially and psychologically hazardous as well.

Which is one risk Gloomy Gus never took. The only All-American in the history of his little college, the first Heisman Trophy winner (I heard at the hospital today from the sportswriter doing that retrospective piece on him that because of his involvement in the Memorial Day riot, there's a move underfoot now to erase his award from the books— but can history be erased? yes, yes, it always is, in fact that's the *first* thing that happens to it . . .), an All-Pro halfback for the NFL Chicago Bears, and it still isn't clear he ever understood what the game is all about at the most fundamental level. Or ever wished to know. Certainly, he had not been attracted to freedom, mystery, beauty—if anything, he was frightened by such things. He apparently lacked any

capacity for joy, so how could he have known these
other things even if he'd encountered them? He
would probably have registered them as some kind
of vexatious disorder, and added yet another calis-
thenic to his schedule.

So what drew him to football in the first place?
I'm not sure. When his brother came through looking for him a couple of weeks after Maxie's party,
I asked him how it had started, and what he said
was: "I think it was because of the challenge. It was
the thing he was worst at. That and getting on with
girls. He used to be good at lots of things. Like
mashing potatoes, for example. Or debate. Studies.
We all thought he was going to be a teacher or a
lawyer. Dick was always reserved. He was the stu-
dious one of the bunch, always doing more reading
while the rest of us were out having fun. But what
he did well, he took no pleasure in, while what he
did badly made him very upset."

"Did he talk about these things?"

"No, he just got tics."

Most of what I've come to know about Gloomy
Gus, I learned from his brother on that surprise
weekend visit and from the Hearst reporter doing
the whatever-happened-to wrap-up. Neither man was
very intelligent and I had to piece a lot of it together myself, but I was helped by the sportswriter's notes and a scrapbook of Gus's football career
that his brother brought along with him, together

with some testimonials from girls he'd had. This brother is a grocer and souvenir seller with his father back in Gus's hometown, and I gathered they'd been cleaning up by playing on Gus's national fame—he showed me a picture of the store and it was full of Chicago Bears programs, pennants, publicity shots, and the like, as well as footballs, jerseys, autographed photos of famous ladies, and other mementos of the Bears' All-Pro halfback. He expressed a great deal of concern for his brother, but it was obvious that underneath he was angry and embarrassed by the way Gus had let him down. "So this is where he's ended up," he said, gazing around my studio. "I never realized Dick had fallen so far . . ."

Apparently, the critical turning point in Gloomy Gus's life came during his freshman year at Whittier College out in southern California. At that moment, he did what sooner or later we all do: he began to simplify himself. I can understand this: my sculpting is not something that was added to an expanding life, but that which remains after all the other things have been peeled away, things that, who knows, I might have been better at. We all have too few lives to live. Later, in an unpublished interview, Gus was to say that all he ever wanted to do was play football and screw girls, but up till that autumn in 1930 he had been trying to score everywhere at once: as a scholar, a politician, an organist, pianist, and violinist, a carny barker, gas station attendant, Quaker Sunday School teacher, debater and actor, entrepreneur, journalist, songwriter and playwright. A familiar pattern: he seemed destined to become president of the local Chamber of Commerce, or maybe a judge. He'd won scholarships, elections, awards, leading roles, oratorical contests, and public praise. But he still hadn't been able to make the football team or coax a girl's underpants down.

Which was more important to him is not clear. In later years, Gus himself spoke mostly about football, but the Hearst guy insists that under the uniform he was "ninety-nine and forty-four one-hundredths percent pure hard-on." Gus's brother had no opinion, though when I asked he winked broadly. This wink was a peculiarity of Gus's brother, however, and could have signified anything. Girls admired Gus apparently, but they didn't have much fun with him. He developed a kind of paranoia, stimulated by some advertisement maybe, about having bad breath—each morning before leaving the house, he used to brush his teeth, gargle with special mouth-washes, and make his mother smell his breath—but at least part of the problem was that on dates he talked to the girls about such things as what might have happened to the world if Persia had conquered the Greeks, and then with no transition tried to wrestle them to the floor. This never worked. Like-wise with the football: it was all verbal. Maybe his early successes with debates and elections had twisted him a bit. One teammate who knew him that freshman year summed up his talents very simply: "Dick had two left feet. He couldn't coor-dinate." Then why was he allowed to go on working out with the team? "He was always talking it up.

That's why the Chief let him hang around. He was one of the inspirational guys." Of course, even the talking had required practice and so, like his acting, was cued and predictable, though maybe people failed to notice this at the time. A kind of religious recitation. We tried him out on winter nights around my stove. If you said, "Keep it rolling," he'd say, "Fuckin' good game!" If you said, "That's showing them," he'd say, "Make 'em eat shit!" Et cet.

The Chief was not an ungenerous man; he might have let Gus play from time to time just to be fair about it. Shut him up maybe. Besides, the Whittier Poets were terrible teams, freshmen and varsity both, they were sure to lose, no matter who played. But Gus suffered from something worse than just the two left feet: uncontrollable overeagerness. Every time he went into the game, he immediately went offside. As he bounded forward, his team marched backward, five penalty yards per play. Even if he was centering the ball himself (the Chief was resourceful, he tried that one too). He just couldn't hold himself back. Girls, too, who might have surrendered to him in a moment of whimsical magnanimity, were put off by the way he lurched out of control before the foreplay had even begun.

There seemed to be no motive behind this overeagerness. It was just a part of him, like the two left feet—it was difficult, in fact, for him to recog-

nize that the fault might be his: he thought the rest
of the world had two right feet and tended to col-
lapse into slow-motion sequences. This characteristic, which was less than zeal but more than a con-
ditioned reflex, may have got a certain amount of
encouragement in his early life, since in other activities less formal than football and courtship it
had served him well—he was like a jack-in-the-box
in classrooms and student assemblies, debates, and
fraternity meetings, and he won everything simply
by astonishing everybody else into silence—but it
was not basically something learned. I don't know
much about his birth (except that the sportswriters
always liked to claim there was an eclipse of the
sun that day), but I wouldn't be surprised to learn
that he came tearing out of his mother's womb well
before she was ready. He had what I can only describe as a short-circuited stimulus–response system in which everything operated on the knee-jerk
principle. He spent most of the last six or seven
years of his life struggling against this flaw, but as
with any fundamental characteristic, the more he
fought it, the more it dominated his life. With me
it's passivity, the open door; with Gloomy Gus, it
was the plunge offside.

What had always worked best for him in his other
activities was his discipline (also innate maybe, a
kind of corollary of the overeagerness, but probably not; maybe his mother stuffed it into him with

her Bible readings)—his careful preparations, self-control, dogged practice—so that's what he turned to now in the fall of 1930 in his effort to overcome his failure on the football field and in the back seats of cars. I say "turned to," "effort to overcome," but I don't mean to suggest there was anything overtly conscious about it. I've tried to imagine what bent him that fall and started him down the path to the Memorial Day massacre at the Republic Steel plant. He seemed uninterested in rewards, popularity, even love or happiness, and he was impervious to ridicule or criticism. Yet, at the same time, he lived in almost freakish immediacy to the world around him, a helpless puppet on a string, elbows akimbo and left feet twitching at every social whim. I don't think he even "wanted" to play football or have sex—it was the world that *told* him he wanted these things, just as it might have told him instead to work for the New Deal, market frozen orange juice, get rich in Cuba, or run for Congress. He was nothing but Self, yet so invaded, more selfless than any of us in a way; without the sense of Audience, he would have been a lifeless pile of sticks and rags. Such a system may be reinforced by rewards and applause, but by small increments only. Only one thing will turn it around: violent disapproval. Fury. Rage. A beating, even. Who tore into him finally? Was it the coach? His heavy-handed father? His girlfriend?

Whoever it was put the fatal twist in his mechanism, that autumn Gloomy Gus made one simple
alteration in his daily pattern, and so commenced
to reshape his destiny: he set aside thirty minutes
every day to practice not going offside. This habit
of scheduling his time was one he'd picked up
early, a consequence of his music lessons maybe.
I've tried it myself from time to time, but I always
misplace the schedules. Besides, somebody can always come through the door and spoil it for me.
Mainly I do it because I enjoy writing out the
schedules, it's a kind of daydreaming. Gus was
more serious about it. At first it had merely been
the way to make full (and as his Quaker grandmother would say, "proper") use of his free time
after school and on weekends, but by the time he
was thirteen the idea of "free time" had faded
from his memory and all twenty-four hours, seven
days a week, were locked up in his timetable. This
meant that when something new was phased in—
the thirty minutes spent learning not to go offside,
for example—something else had to get squeezed
or cut altogether. It was at this time that he gave
up writing songs for his fraternity ("All hail the
mighty boar, / Our patron beast is he . . . ," this
was one of his famous ones) and mashing potatoes
for his mother. This potato-mashing, incidentally,
was not as irrelevant as it might seem. His mother
once said of his skills (this made all the newspa-

pers): "He never left any lumps. He used the whipping motion to make them smooth instead of going up and down the way the other boys did." But since nothing ever came naturally to him, it's obvious he'd had to devote a good part of his childhood working up this talent, one of his first to be noticed. Again inspired by a burst of anger, no doubt—his father is a moody, hot-blooded Black Irishman, handy with the razor strop, and he's never liked lumpy mashed potatoes. Thus, an early establishment of the pattern, and Gus had evidently clung to this potato-mashing exercise like a security blanket up to that autumn of his freshman year in college.

His brother described Gus's freshman year as one of the worst of his—the brother's—life. Gus's other pursuits had been essentially private ones, but now with this offside problem he needed others to help, and his younger brother got the brunt of it. At first Gus did try to go it alone, using an alarm clock, but the ring was too much like the school bell, and it made him very jumpy in classrooms: he sometimes found himself out of his seat five minutes before the bell and down in a crouch in the front of the room, tense with expectation. So he got his brother to call numbers. Arbitrarily, they chose "29" as the signal to go. I asked the brother why and he said: "I don't know. The year maybe."

"You mean, because of the crash?"

"No, it was 1930, remember, and I think we

thought that '29' would cause just that split second of delay that Dick needed. It was a mistake, though."

"A mistake?"

"Using just one number like that. We realized too late we should have mixed them up. He never quite got over it. You know what they say, the things you learn first stick with you the longest. Every time somebody shouted '29' after that, he was off and running. Had to leave it out of the signals, and even the Bears, you know, had to be sure not to call an accidental '29.' It was supposed to be kept secret, but somehow it leaked out, and that leak was part of what got him in trouble finally."

The half-hour-a-day practice paid off. A couple of weeks after he'd begun the exercise, the Chief gave him another chance. It was late in the game and the freshman Poets were trailing by five touchdowns. The Poets' left tackle got hit hard and the Chief sent Gus in for one play, sacrificing the expected five-yard offside penalty loss, while the other guy got his wind back. The play was called and for the first time in his football career Gus managed to stay down until the ball was snapped. But he got smeared. They had to carry him off the field on a stretcher. As they passed the Chief with him, he looked up with a hopeful smile and asked: "How'd I do, Coach?"

The Chief looked down at this eager, curlyheaded kid, whose face was presently all chopped up with cleat marks, and said grimly: "Well, at least you didn't go offside."

"Gosh . . . thanks, Chief!"

"*Thanks*—! Thanks for *what?* You were *terrible!* You let that worthless sonofabitch walk right over you! Instead of five yards, we lost *fifteen!*"

Gus looked rattled. "But . . . what . . . what did I do wrong?"

The coach stared down at him in disbelief, shook his head. "Well, for one thing, son," he sighed (on the field a pass had been intercepted, the Poets were now six touchdowns behind), "keep your butt down. You're not up there to blow farts, you're part of a wall and your ass is the weight that's holding it up. And when I say you gotta be on your toes, I don't mean like a goddamn ballet dancer—*dig in!* Become *part* of that turf you're holding! And your fingers—look at 'em! They're all bloodied up! Three of 'em look broken! Don't spread 'em out like that! Knuckle under, make 'em into fists, flexible but hard! And keep your goddamn stupid head down, for Chrissake! It don't matter to you what's behind the guy in front of you, you just hunch your shoulders down and keep an eye on *him!* Watch all of him, but don't let his face take your mind off the important parts: his hands and his knees. That first guy who hit you came in awful high, right at the belly, a very bad habit—lift your knees up when he does that and cure him of it! Now, didja ever think what a shoulder was for? When you— My God, *now* what's the matter? What're you makin' all them damn twitches for?"

"That's . . . that's a lot to remember, Chief . . ."

But Gloomy Gus was nothing if not thorough. He added an hour and forty minutes to his daily schedule, giving up the playwriting, glee club, the violin, and pumping gas at his dad's filling station, and set about learning all the things the Chief had told him. Now he needed an opponent as well as someone to call the signals. His brother balked, but got dragged into it just the same. So did his fraternity brothers, neighbors, teammates, even his mother and his girlfriend. His mother showed that Quaker forbearance she was famous for, even when flat out on the field and run over, but his girlfriend quit him, bawling all the way home that she was afraid she was never going to have a baby all her life. His father loved physical contact, but not when it was two-sided, so he steered clear. When Gus couldn't find willing opponents, he used the school tackling dummies, but it was hard to watch the hands and knees. Everything went well enough and he even got into another game before his freshman season ended, performing well on the line. But the coach made the mistake of using him at fullback for one play, and when the quarterback turned around to hand off the ball, Gus creamed him. His own quarterback. "He came in high, Chief—and like you said . . ." The coach hoped the silly bastard would flunk out or get pregnant or something before the next season rolled around.

Speaking of which, he was at this same time working on his problem with girls. Well, not precisely at the same time, since the practice times were in different parts of his daily schedule. Which accounted for his picking up girlfriends in one season and losing them in the next. His technique was precisely the same: learn one thing at a time, starting with the simplest, and practice it over and over and over until it was second nature (there being no first with Gus, of course). Then add the next element. As with football, he began by learning how not to go offside, though the problem here was slightly different. In effect, he had to unlearn what he knew or thought he knew about sex and start over with holding hands. For thirty minutes every day, he practiced going through the Persians-and-Greeks thing, then reaching for the girl's hand. It was not always easy to find girls to practice this with. His brother said he hated this part even more than being a tackling dummy. Especially since Gus was a slow learner and kept making appalling mistakes. But then it occurred to him one day that he didn't need the Persians and Greeks anymore, and with that it became easier to find willing girls again, though they never understood the constant repeats and the abrupt dismissals when the thirty minutes were up.

Over the months that followed, he continued his exercises, expanding them to include new techniques picked up from coaches, friends, movies, books, teammates, barbershops, parents, and burlesque shows in Los Angeles. He learned how— each in separate drills—to tackle and block, swear vehemently, break out of a huddle, cradle a ball, throw it and catch it and inflate it, how to squeeze hands, caress them, gaze deeply, joke casually, wink, blow loose wisps of hair back, ask for a phone number, stand tall, and even foxtrot a bit. Not without paying a price, of course. Something had to go to make room for all of this. He was able to compress some practice times, once he'd mastered a given skill, but he discovered he could not omit any drill altogether or the skills slipped away from him again. Even the offside practice: he got it down to about two minutes a day, but he couldn't get rid of it. And one skill did not simply lead to another—more often it led to a dozen, and each of these dozen to a dozen each, multiplying like leaves on a fast-branching tree. I could understand his dilemma. I have the same problem with my sculpting: I can never hope to catch up. I'm afraid we had a lot in common, Gloomy Gus and I, more than I've sometimes wished to admit. I've said we simplified ourselves—but didn't we merely substitute a vertical madness for a horizontal one?

Moreover, in Gus's case, the various responses with which opposing teams and girls might confront him were virtually infinite—relatively, with my inert bits of metal, I have it easy—and, lacking any instinct for either discipline, he had to learn them all, one by one, and then memorize countermoves, a stupendous task that only one as disciplined as Gloomy Gus could ever have undertaken. It was made all the more complex by his belief (or maybe it was instinct, same source as the offside lurch) in the surprise counterattack as the only possible reply: "You cannot win a battle in any arena of life merely by defending yourself." He felt that, since girls and football teams are "not intelligent, but stupid, it is important whenever possible to confront them with an unexpected maneuver." There's a famous maxim, attributed to him, on the subject: "Take the offensive, show no fear, do the unexpected, but do nothing rash!" But since all his moves were studied out and practiced, how could they be surprises? This became his master task: to make the response mechanism so intricate that the patterns were invisible. A million new drills, then, and to make room for them, he had to abandon his music, fraternity, edifying outside reading, hamburger-grinding, presidency of Christian Endeavor, baseball and tennis, oratory, school newspaper editorship, friendly conversations, and Latin club. Though he cut back sharply on the time spent on acting and debate, he clung to them, as well as to his campus politics and studies, the latter because he had to pass his courses to stay in school and play football, the others because they doubled as verbal calisthenics for lockerroom banter and picking up new girls.

While to the casual observer the results of all this rigor and sacrifice may not have been spectacular, they were nevertheless impressive enough. Before classes had begun next fall, to the surprise of the coach he had made the varsity football squad, and to the surprise of the head cheerleader had gently sucked her left pap. In fact, he had sucked it three times in succession, starting from scratch with the wink, pickup, and handholding each time through, and all she could think of to say was: "Don't you like the other one?" "He looked so surprised," she said after, "that I don't think he knew there *was* another one." On the football field he was neither brilliant nor imaginative, but he was consistent. The coach still didn't trust him in the backfield, but he did let him play right end in the second half of the fourth game of the season. He did well, staying onside until the ball was centered, taking out his man, throwing textbook blocks, and running convincing decoys, until on about the seventh or eighth play he was thrown a pass. He floated far out on the right flank, shook off his opponent, sprinted downfield, turned at just the right moment, leaped gracefully, and made a phenomenal catch of a wobbling, overthrown pass—the students and fans in the stands went wild. But when he came down, he just stood there, smiling blankly. For a moment, everybody on the field was like that, stopped dead, staring at him, dumbfounded. Then they hit him. So hard in fact that he fumbled the ball, the opponents recovering. Once again, they had to carry him off.

"What the hell happened?" cried the coach as they carried him by, in pain but still smiling.

"I couldn't remember what came next, Chief," he said.

The coach was nearly crying, but what he said was: "Y'know, if they'd had more guys like you in the cavalry, maybe we wouldn'ta been the ones to end up on the goddamn reservations!"

"Gosh . . . thanks, Coach . . ."

Gus, when he was able, went back to the practice field. Fields. He no longer had time for campus politics, little theater, or debate society. Every minute in his daily timetable not used for eating, sleeping, toilet, and classwork went into learning everything there was to know about girls and football. He'd had an experience with a girl from his chemistry class much like the one he'd had on the football field: he'd got her skirts up all right and knew what the equivalent of a touchdown was, but he'd forgotten to practice getting an erection. He'd expanded his practice schedule, apparently determined never to let these things happen again, although his brother said he didn't think it was determination. He thought it was more like grabbing a tiger's tail: no conscious decisions, just one desperate thing after another. "One fact you oughta understand," he told me as we sat in my back room looking through the scrapbook (he'd turned down a cup of coffee after seeing the condition of my pot), "when Dick was three years old he fell out of a buggy and the iron wheel ran over his head— he's got a scar from the top of his forehead to the back of his neck from it." The brother's suspicion that Gus wasn't all there I shared, but I didn't think the bump had anything to do with it.

Whatever moved him—his own inspiration or mere mechanics—he set about to master the two arts once and for all. He not only drilled himself on all aspects of offense and defense, of foreplay and conquest, but he also had practice sessions on how to jog out onto the field, spit water during time-outs, laugh at the coach's jokes, and crack bare butts with wet towels in the showerroom (his brother balked at practicing this one with him, and even his mother's Christian forbearance failed her before he'd got the knack), how to compliment girls' private parts politely in public, avoid entangling alliances, take a slap, test condoms, dance the Charleston, and recognize jazz-babies, red-hot mamas, and virgins by the way they walked. By the time the football season rolled around his junior year, he'd been named the second-string right half-back by the coach of the Whittier Poets and jerked off by the captain of the women's volleyball team, both of whom admitted later to a lot of preliminary soul-searching.

The only remarkable thing about the first few games of that 1932 season was that nothing went radically wrong. Drills and exercises were one thing, real games were another, and Gus hadn't put it all together yet, but he had set aside seventy-five minutes a day with three hours extra on weekends for what he called "meshing sessions," and by the fourth or fifth game it was all beginning to fall into place. He wasn't fast as a runner, but he was nimble, deceptive, and hard-hitting, a tricky man to bring down. His pass reception was sure-fingered, if a bit stiff in its orthodoxy, and his defensive play was sometimes crude but always effective. He could pass when he had to (though he didn't seem to like releasing the ball once he had it in his hands—sometimes people even had to take it away from him to center it for the next play), and he was very impressive at reading offensive plays of the opponent, slapping butts in huddles, and coming on and off the field. Finally, after a lot of soul-searching, the coach decided to start him for the Homecoming Game.

It was a beautiful southern California day in mid-November, and the Whittier stands were filled with alumni, disgruntled by the recent elections and back on campus for what they assumed was to be another punishing humiliation for their alma mater. They wanted to fire the coach, but they doubted they could find anyone else who would take the job. Mrs. Herbert Hoover, wife of the defeated President and a former student of this Quaker college, was said to be present, but this did not appreciably raise any spirits. There was a parade on the field before the game, to be followed by the crowning of the Homecoming Queen, who would then preside over the game and other festivities of the day, if "festivities" was the word for such a dismal Quaker program. Since she had a little prayer to deliver during the ceremony, the Queen-elect slipped behind the bleachers at one of the endzones for a moment to practice, and there she bumped into Gloomy Gus. This was his first game as a starter, so he was back there squeezing in fifteen quick minutes of flag-saluting drill to prepare himself for the playing of "The Star-Spangled Banner." He glanced up, smiling absently, then a flicker of recognition came to his eyes, his

113

lips parted, he smiled gently, tilting his head just so, and said: "Priscilla! Priscilla, I've been looking for you!" Then he took her hand . . .

By the time the Homecoming Queen staggered out onto the field, starry-eyed, badly rumpled, and bloodstained in the rear, the ceremonies were over. The president of the college, in desperation, had named Mrs. Hoover the honorary Homecoming Queen, but then it had turned out she wasn't in the stands after all. The alumni had taken it all in their stride, business as usual, and passed around their flasks of bathtub gin. In a couple of short seasons, they'd suffered a stock-market crash, the outbreak of war in Manchuria, the kidnapping of the Lindbergh baby, a Bonus March by a lot of ex-enlisted riffraff on Washington, and the defeat of the Republican Party—what was a mere assault on their Homecoming Queen? They settled back to watch their football team get taken apart once again, hoping only that the gin held out.

The Poets always fumbled the opening kickoff, it was a Homecoming tradition. But in 1932 the tradition was broken. Gloomy Gus hauled the ball in and ran eighty-five yards through the entire opposition for a touchdown, the first of his career. So spectacular was it, the fans just sat there in stunned silence. Gus had this knack for leaving people with their jaws hanging open, I've witnessed it myself. This silence rattled him for a moment and he may have wondered if they'd noticed he had his pants on inside out. But then they erupted in wild cheering, screaming, foot-stamping. Old men rushed out onto the field to hug him, kiss him, lift him on their shoulders, even though there was still a whole game to play. And what a game. He scored seven touchdowns all by himself in the first half. The coach finally had to take him out of the game so the other team would go on playing. He let him back in for the last three minutes of the game because the alumni had been throatily demanding it, and he scored yet again on three straight power plays. It was a school record. The whole town went delirious with joy. Luckily, he'd practiced riding around on shoulders and receiving accolades, maybe in fact it was one of the first things he'd practiced, so he carried himself elegantly as long as it lasted. The Homecoming Queen lay in the supply room, taking on anyone who'd approach her in the plain speech. The coach put on Indian feathers and led a dance. Everybody told him he was a genius. The party went on for three days, though Gus, of course, had long since withdrawn—as soon as he'd come down off the shoulders, in fact—in order to stick to his timetable.

Now that he was playing first-team football and having it off with girls regularly, there were some adjustments in his practice schedules, but it did not get easier for him. He still had to preserve all the old drills, and now there were new subtleties to learn, new plays on the field, new challenges from girls. He had to learn to cope with various forms of intercourse hysteria, for example, and to talk with sports reporters, address student rallies without running for office, pose for photos. The coach, too, had things to learn, such as to leave well enough alone. In the very next game, for example, after Gus had scored four touchdowns in the first quarter, he instructed him to "take it easy, killer," and nearly paralyzed him. Then the Chief tried to take over Gus's entire practice schedule—partly, it should be said, because Gus's mother and brother begged the coach to be relieved of this burden once and for all—and he made the mistake, in spite of the brother's warnings, of canceling or just ignoring some of the fundamental drills, such as how to turn while running, how to fade back for a pass, how to hunker down, ball the fists, break from a huddle, and so on. The result of this was that Gus spun into illegal motion the first ten plays of the next game. The coach was wild with panic. He kept pinching himself in the face and shaking his head. Gus's brother came to the rescue.

"I took Dick out behind the bleachers for fifteen minutes of offside drill. It was just luck I drilled him that long, any more I couldn't have taken, but a minute less and it wouldn't have been enough. We didn't find this out right away, but it turned out if he missed any practice time, he had to make it up completely. He could cut fat from the schedule, but not any single increment of it. He'd gone a week, seven days, without his offside drill, and at two minutes a day that meant he was fourteen minutes behind. All I knew that day was that suddenly he seemed to get it and I was barely able to walk. I told the coach: 'I think he's all right.'

"We were losing 14–0 at this point—it would've been worse, but luckily we were up against one of the worst teams in the circuit—so the coach rushed him back into the game. He didn't go offside, but that was the only thing he didn't do wrong. He seemed to understand the plays, but his legs didn't work. His mind seemed to be racing ahead and his body made motions they would have made forty yards downfield, but his feet were rooted to the spot. Sometimes he didn't even get turned around and facing the right direction after a huddle. The coach was in a terrible funk. He'd begun to think he might get invited to coach at some school where they paid real money and had real football players, maybe even the Ivy League or the pros, and so he was frantic that Dick was blowing it for him. I tried to help, but the Chief was completely incoherent and kept making strange Indian noises, and I was afraid he was going to take out on me what he was feeling toward Dick.

"At halftime, though, I was able to get through to the Chief. We were behind by four or five touchdowns by then, and the coach couldn't even talk. He kept his Indian feathers in the lockerrooms now for celebrations, and he just sat there eating them. We all thought he'd had a stroke. I asked to see Dick's practice schedule for the past week. I studied it over and said: 'I think he can still throw passes if somebody will tuck the ball in his hands.' I'll never forget the look on the Chief's face, Meyers. It was one of those moments when you think either you or the rest of the world has to be crazy, and you're no longer so sure you're the one who's all right. He swallowed the feathers he was eating and said in a throaty whisper: 'Throw? Passes?' 'It's not what he does best,' I said, 'but you've ruined him for anything else.' This hit the Chief very hard, I felt sorry for him, but he knew it was true.

"Well, he was grasping for straws at this point, so rather than quit or scalp us both, he took the chance. What did he have to lose? I took Dick out behind the stands again for fifteen minutes of practicing feints and breaking out of the huddle. I hoped this would loosen him up and that some of the other skills would come back to him in the course of the game. It didn't matter, after all, where he did his practicing, on the field or off. Anyway, it worked. It wasn't Dick's most brilliant day maybe, passing was something he never completely perfected, and the Poets didn't have anybody who could catch the ball, but he hit them squarely enough so that they managed to score a touchdown and only fumbled or got intercepted half a dozen times. More important, I told the coach to repeat plays over and over like a kind of drill. This was completely against the Chief's instincts, of course, but he had no choice. This worked, too. It was the same as practice time for Dick, and his legs slowly came back to him. We lost the game, but the last eight minutes of it were so fantastic it felt like victory. Dick played both offense and defense and he scored three times in those eight minutes. They tried to stall, but Dick hit them so hard it was impossible for them to

119

hang on to the ball. You know, Meyers, when my brother was good, there was nothing in the whole goddamn world he couldn't fuck over!"

The last two games of the season were apparently real bloodlettings. The scrapbook showed he made the front page of nearly every newspaper in California. The coach probably should have taken Gus out after he got eight or nine touchdowns ahead, but he was too shaky to do anything by then but let things happen by themselves. They were such unsporting devastations that a number of teams canceled the next season's games with Whittier. The coach was disconcerted by this boycott, but managed to turn it to his own advantage, filling the 1933 schedule with big-name teams. These teams had everything to lose and nothing to gain, so it wasn't easy to draw them into a game, but he did get Notre Dame, which was also having trouble finding opponents in those days, and more important, though less of a team, Washington and Jefferson. Both wanted to use Whittier as a warm-up, early in the season, which spoiled the Chief's sense of dramatic climax, but this, too, turned out well in the end. The stunning defeat of Notre Dame put Whittier in the national newspapers, and Gus's massacre of Washington and Jefferson was so fearsome that the visitors not only refused to finish the game, leaving in utter self-disgust after the score reached 76–0, but they gave up football for the rest of the season, allowing Whittier to take over their program. By the time the Homecoming Game with Duke rolled around that year, Mrs. Herbert Hoover *was* in attendance, and the new Homecoming Queen was waiting tremulously outside the players' lockerroom an hour before the opening ceremonies. Gloomy Gus broke almost every offensive record in the books that season, as did the Poets, though their record was more or less identical to his—the only important records left standing, in fact, were for punts and field goals, simply because the Poets never had to fall back on them.

Our paths might have crossed that fall and winter. Pursued by history, I was on the bum, drifting westward to California. Gus, making what I was running from, was being brought east to be wined and dined by the professionals. I was traveling on freights or hitchhiking ("goosing the ghost," as Jesse calls it, a bit of slang left over from his days as a Bible salesman), he came first class by the *Rocket*. They took him to the National Football League championship between the Chicago Bears and the New York Giants, which the Bears won, 23–21, and to the Chicago Century of Progress Exposition. I sometimes felt that it was the insane preparations for that tinsely fair, in the middle of so much human misery, that had elbowed me out of Chicago, but I would have envied him his trip on the Skyride.

He was already famous and became more a part of the fair than a visitor. He and Sally Rand and the Enchanted Island. While I, feeling exiled from myself and having had to sneak past border vigilantes and escape from detention camps, was out in southern California, partly because I'd hoped to reach Mexico, a private pilgrimage to the murals (didn't make it), mainly just because it was warmer. You didn't freeze sleeping in the street. I worked my way from town to town as an odd-jobs man, wearing cardboard in the soles of my shoes, and on my back whatever gratuities fell there. In the Los Angeles area, some stern old lady gave me a moth-eaten sweater with some kind of fraternity insignia on it, and for all I know she was Gus's grandmother. In Chicago, Gus seduced an entire cross section of the city on a one-each-of-a-kind program, and as far as he knew one of them was my sister. If I'd had a sister. Each day he practiced religiously, protecting and honing his skills and adding new ones. I was adding new ones, too— plumbing, carpentry, gardening, bricklaying, automobile repair, electrical wiring, even begging and petty thievery—and though my hunger was more immediate and familiar, it could be said that hunger drove us both. Both of us were ranging far from home, fulfilling myths about ourselves, his the rags-to-riches drama of the industrious American boy, mine the curse of the Wandering Jew.

And we were both—captives of alienating systems—divided within ourselves. "To subdivide a man," Marx has said, "is to execute him if he deserves the sentence, to assassinate him if he does not."

At home, I find that somebody's painted a swastika on my door with black paint. Some childish prank probably, but that doesn't stop my heart from leaping to my throat. I try to stare as coldly as I can at the thing, since maybe they're watching me to see what I'll do, but inside I feel like I'm coming apart at all the joints. I'm an atheist, my first struggle against ideology was against Judaism, Freud freed me from my family, what was left of it, and socialism from my parochialism, but it's all been an illusion, I can see that now. Meyer, I say to myself, feeling again that jerk on the leash, be a Jew. Stop kidding yourself, and be a Jew.

I step firmly toward the door (have I been thinking about walking away, pretending I don't live here?) and force the key in. Then suddenly I get panicky about the Baron. Of course, the Baron isn't Jewish. But kids in the neighborhood have tried to get him before. I burst into my studio, arms full of fish and fruit, calling for him. He comes in from the back, stretching sleepily, rubs up against my leg to be stroked. "Hey, Baron," I cry, setting the packages down. "That's all right, boy, it ain't the last consumption!" Something Jesse used to say after a bad day on the road. The Baron sniffs the groceries. I'm calming down at last. I give the Baron the fishheads and other scraps. I'd meant to parcel them out over two or three meals, but I'm so grateful he's alive, I give it all up at once like some kind of propitiating sacrifice. Be a Jew.

"There was much that was interesting and much that was amusing in our house," Gorky wrote, "but sometimes I was overwhelmed by a vast longing. It was as though a great burden were weighing me down, and I went on living at the bottom of an inky pit, bereft of sight and hearing and feeling—blind and only half alive." For over a month, that's how I've felt. "Confined in a cold oily bubble . . . stuck into it like a midge." But no longer. Now, with that swastika on the door, the Baron rumbling softly over the stringy translucent bits, blind Gorky looking down on me, Gus dead and the streets drying up, my clothes wet on me and abrasive, dust motes floating in the soft ivory glow this side of the front window, I know that dead time is over. I'm frightened, but I'm alive again. And I know something else: I'm not going to Spain. Or to Palestine either. No more abdications. On some open shelving just past Gorky's square chin lies some of my early work, bits and pieces of unfinished ideas, a few blasted victims from the Guernica blitz, odd scraps of collected junk, all heaped up on each other. There is no harmony in this random pile, but there is life. I don't like Jane Addams' carved wooden head lying there on that scarred steel clutch plate, but in its harsh dissonance the juxtaposition seems to say more about life than her head alone—romanticized, yes, I know that, but sometimes you can't help it—ever did. Somebody has draped upon a Medusa-like crown of welded hair—but faceless—an old cap I used to wear on the road, and in the empty space where the face should be, like a kind of nose, leans the upraised leg of a baseball pitcher. I sit back against a bucket of scrap metal, thinking: In a class-ridden society, although itineraries may pass by and over each other, there is no real intersection—it's like separate planes sliding by each other. Now I want to make them collide. It will be uncomfortable, but I want to do this. Why am I trying to express harmony and simplicity when that isn't what I feel?

The swastika is still on the door and on my mind. The door I've left open, folded back against the inner wall, not wanting to put the sign out, so to speak, but I can't leave it that way. I could scrape it off, but they'd probably just paint it on again. Paint over it, same thing. Besides, whatever the intentions of those who put it there, it has come to me as a kind of sign, and I feel like it's important to leave it there. Transfigured maybe, but not dismissed. Never throw nothin' away. I go get some black paint and turn the swastika into three little squares, leaving the fourth, the upper left one, open. The two squares adjacent to the open one I fill with sprays of colored flowers cut from a little book of them I have, and the other square I paint red. The irony of the flowers is submerged maybe in the implied cowardice in failing to declare myself (where are the Star of David, working-class symbols, or laments for bloodied Spain?), but in the land of the wolves things are bad enough without putting out bait. Especially when you're the little pig who lives in the straw house. Or so I explain to the Baron, while varnishing the flowers.

I'm just finishing the last panel when Harry's sister Golda arrives with a paring knife in her hand. "I seen it when I went by earlier, Meyer. I come back to scrape it off." She seems pretty shaken. Of course, she's been through a lot of late. "It's terrible, Meyer. What's happening to our people?"

"Don't let it upset you, Golda. Just kids, probably."

"I'll be honest, when I first seen it there I looked the other way and run off. Then I got mad at myself and so I come back."

"I know. I nearly couldn't open the door at

first. But it's okay now," I say, smiling up at her. She looks older than she has recently, worn down, vulnerable. "Golda, listen, I'm sorry. I just came from the hospital. Gus is dead."

"I know. Harry called me after he seen you." She sighs heavily, holding one breast. "People are wonderful, Meyer, they can get used to everything in this world." The very words no doubt of our brethren in the German ghettos, streets of Guernica, hills of Ethiopia. It's a sentiment neither Gorky nor I much admire, but have learned to live with, even in ourselves, as though to acknowledge its universality. "I like the flowers," she says. "But . . . still it's scary. You can't forget what's underneath."

"That's sort of the idea, Golda." I tell her about the fresh strawberries and she goes back to my room to wash them while I clean out my brush. She notices my wet clothes and makes me take them all off. She hangs them outside, while I change into dry underwear, thick socks, and a sweater. I don't have a second pair of pants.

What with all this domesticity, the fruity perfume of the strawberries (she's put them in a little vinegar and sugar to bring the juices out), the day's stresses, the memories the room holds for Golda, and the essential loneliness we both share, we soon find ourselves tumbling about on the ceremonial cot together. I apologize that I don't have Gus's technique and can't do what he did for her, but she laughs sadly and says it's all illusion anyhow, just a trick of the imagination. She coaches me in a few gimmicks she's picked up from Gloomy Gus and seems to have a good time. Afterwards, having kissed all my bruises, even the ones on my behind ("battle wounds," she calls them, licking at them tenderly, respectfully), she hugs me close and says she was very satisfied, and I can't complain. My Homecoming Queen. I'm afraid she's going to ask me why I don't have a girlfriend, and that's exactly what she does. "A healthy boy like you, Meyer . . ."

"I like to be alone, Golda."

She's quiet for a moment. "Do you want to be alone now?"

"No," I lie. "No, this is great." How did Gloomy Gus do it, I wonder. Just in and out and never look back: that's the coaching I really need. "But I do have to be alone a lot, and it's hard for girls to understand that."

"You've had girls living with you, Meyer?"

"Sometimes. I've always liked having them around, but it's never worked out. They sit in the studio reading a book, insisting they won't bother me, but of course they already are. They try painting while I sculpt—I'm very weak, it's their paintings I spend the day with. I build up to my best work all day, but just then I hear them frying something on the stove. I can't let it get cold, can I? The minute the thought crosses my mind, I've lost my momentum. On the very best days, I rarely get more than twenty or thirty perfect minutes, the rest all preparations and reflections, and with all the best intentions, they've taken these moments away from me. It's always hard to tell them to go away and leave me alone for a while—and sometimes I mean for several days, even weeks—in fact, it's the hardest thing of all. Almost I can't do it. So finally I've found it best to avoid the problem. For now, anyway."

"The trouble is, Meyer," she says softly, "you've never been in love."

"Why do you say that?"

"Because it's always 'they,' not 'she.' "

"That's just my shyness, Golda, in talking about it."

"But don't you get lonely sometimes?"

"Sure."

"Meyer, I won't bother you, I promise. But when you get lonely, call me up, okay?"

"Okay, Golda. But—"

She presses her finger on my lips. "I know, I know," she says. "Let's have some strawberries."

She seems calmer now, almost happy. We sit on the edge of the cot in our underwear, munching the bright-red strawberries and talking cheerfully about Gloomy Gus. I describe the scene down at the hospital, she tells me about the last time he made love to her. It was just like all the other times until she asked him if it was the only way he knew, and—whirr-*click!*—he switched tracks and treated her to a feast of oral sex unlike anything she'd ever known before.

"You mean sixty-nine?"

"Yeah, well," she grins, strawberry juice trickling out the corners of her mouth, "I didn't take no more chances with numbers . . ."

The one thing she couldn't get used to, she says, was how inconsistent he was: desperately in love with her one moment, utterly indifferent the next. "He was just a gay deceiver, Meyer," she sighs.

"Well," I smile, "more like a coldhearted craftsman, I'm afraid. One thing he always said in interviews: 'What determines success or failure is the ability to keep coldly objective when emotions are running high.' He isolated himself from his feelings through discipline. He lived life in a kind of time-tunnel. Every minute of every day he lived was completely used up in working on his skills, even when he seemed to be simply enjoying them."

"He did seem very serious . . ."

"I work pretty hard, Golda, but next to him I'm a complete amateur. I wouldn't be surprised if even his dreams were training programs. Maybe that was where he kept up the old skills he'd learned before giving them up for football and girls."

"He always told me he dreamed of me, Meyer," she whispers, gazing lovingly upon a plump red strawberry, the best of the box. "Probably it was just sweet nothings, hunh? Salting me up . . ."

"You know, I don't think he knew what love was all about—or football either. He'd taught himself how to score, but after he'd scored he didn't know what to do but score again."

"I know. A girl just didn't know where she was with him . . ."

"He was very skillful, Golda, but he was a man without an overview. He lived this rigid, segmented, repetitive life, and he couldn't step back. His inability to discriminate was phenomenal. He was a freak, all willpower, no judgment—"

"You mean," she muses, strawberry juice dribbling down her soft chin, "he was a eager beaver who couldn't see past the end of his own shnozzle . . ."

"You could say so," I smile. "You know, people complain we don't live enough in the here and now. Either we're absorbed in the past or daydreaming about the future, which is presumably a very crazy way to behave, because we're missing the real thing and taking the imaginary thing as real. 'Live like each moment is your last,' they say."

"They're right, Meyer. It's the truth."

"But that was just how Gus lived, though without the morbid touch: moment by moment, each out cut off from the next, fulfilling his timetable. We talk about living in the present because we can't imagine actually doing it. He did it. He was in that sense the perfect realist, the absolute materialist."

"He was a lot smarter than me, I know that."

"We think of the past and the future as part of a kind of river, a time-stream, but this is just a poetic metaphor. Gus had no perception of this or any other metaphor. He was completely metaphor-free. He had no imagination at all!"

"Well, I don't know about that," she replies. "Did I ever tell you about his little tricks with the ketchup and cottage cheese?"

"Oh, he was inventive. He had to be. Everything was a crisis for him. Whenever he encountered something new, he tested out responses to it. When something worked, he moved it into his practice schedule and turned it into a habit."

"He had a cute thing with a bicycle pump, too. You should have such habits, Meyer," she teases, popping a strawberry into my mouth. "Sometimes, though, he got very dirty talking, you wouldn't do that . . ."

"Probably he was just getting his line for making out muddled up with his lockerroom banter. Tell me, did he ever hit you with a wet towel?"

"How—how did you know?"

133

"Just a guess . . ."

"I turn my back once to get undressed, that's all, and I'm just pushing down my, my underthings, thinking how excited he must be to see, you know . . . when—oh! What a spank! I thought I would die!"

"It was one of his football exercises, Golda."

"You mean, he wasn't mad—?"

"Not like you mean. He just couldn't keep things straight finally. That was how he cracked up."

"He *was* a little peculiar, Meyer, I know what you're talking about. Once we were hugging and I just squatted down a little so to sit on the bed, when he claps me hard on the tushie and says: 'Let's go git them fuckin' assholes!'—pardon the French, Meyer. And then he turns and runs—*patsch!*—right into the wall!"

"He was breaking out of a huddle . . ."

"He sure was! I thought he was killing himself! I didn't think it was for love, but I couldn't be sure. I run over to help him. I says: 'Dick! Dick! What have you done?' And you know what he says?"

" 'Golda! Golda! I've been looking for you!' "

"You're right, Meyer! That's it! The whole shtick, right from the start, like nothing has happened!"

"It was that routine that ended his career, Golda."

"You mean—? I *thought* there was a woman behind it!" she exclaims, setting her jaw. Then she
sighs. "Tell me the truth, Meyer, there were other
women, weren't there? I mean . . . more than
one . . ."

"Yes, yes, there were, Golda," I say, not wanting to hurt her, but wishing her to be free of this
freak once and for all. "Hundreds, in fact. Every
year."

She takes it better than I expected. Or worse:
it seems to please her. "Was he really so famous,
then?"

"For one season he was the greatest halfback
in football," I say. "He had a secret. But it was
the wrong kind of secret. When he finally went,
it was a terrible thing to watch." So I told her about
all the practice sessions, how he developed his fabulous techniques, demanding ever more and more
of himself, and how these techniques helped him
to score on and off the field like nobody had ever
scored before. "There was no stopping him. It
looked easy, nobody guessed how hard he worked.
In fact, it *was* fairly easy as long as he was in
college. But the big leagues were something else—
just not the same thing as college Homecoming
Queens and Whittier Poets. What he'd learned so
far was just baby stuff. He had to double up on
everything. Getting rid of the classwork was a
help—in fact, he quit right after the football sea-

son was over. He still graduated, but it was mostly on reputation and his personal correspondence with Mrs. Hoover. And in the pros he had a whole team to work with and no longer had to play defense as well as offense. But there were scores of new plays to learn on the field, scores of new positions off. Even the football that season had a new shape, and women in Chicago wore more clothes. Nothing was easy. And of course he couldn't leave out anything he'd learned so far without blowing the works. He even turned his meals into practice sessions for testimonial dinners, pickups, biting in pileups, and muff-diving, so as not to lose time. He—"

"What diving?"

"You know, with the mouth—"

"Oh! I thought you said *muff*-diving . . ."

"I did, Golda. A muff's, you know, for keeping your hands warm—"

"Ah!" she says, blushing, and puts my hand between her legs.

"The point is, in order to keep up with these new demands, even his eating, sleeping, and toilet time had to be used for practice somehow. He hired professionals to sleep with him at night, for example, waking him for five-minute practice sessions at one, three, and five A.M. Even his urination doubled as a drill for flag-saluting during the playing of the National Anthem. It sounds a bit crazy, but the results were good. By the middle of that autumn he was scoring approximately once every eleven minutes on the field and had progressed in his seductions beyond mere movie stars and teammates' wives, into Congress, convents, industrial baronies, and the American Bible Society. On the gridiron, the Bears were unbeatable as long as he was in the lineup, though as the season wore on it got more difficult for him. Now and then he missed a day of practice—once with hay fever, a second time with a wrenched knee, another when he got drugged by a lady psychiatrist who couldn't bear to let him go."

"Oi, I know just how she felt, Meyer . . . !"

"Well, his timetable had been reduced by then to the bare-bone essentials, so to catch up he had to cut more and more into his sleeping time. He was spending as much as eighteen to twenty hours a day at what he called in an interview that 'tough, grinding discipline that is absolutely necessary for superior performance.' Actually, he didn't mind the sleepless nights and even began to believe in them. But then the other teams started filming his play and soon discovered a number of seemingly fixed patterns. They began to predict and intercept his moves. The Bears' coach, seeing Gus was getting outguessed, told him he was too mechanical, he had to think faster on his feet. So he set aside time each day to practice thinking, which meant he had to give up everything subsequent to scoring: no more acknowledgments of applause, no more gratitude to girls. His thinking sessions were essentially efforts to crossbreed all the things he already knew, creating a greatly augmented number of variations on a theme, so to speak. There were still patterns, he couldn't help that, but they were much harder to detect and predict. It was enough to get the Bears through a perfect season in the Western Division, the only one in NFL history, but already by the last game or two the other teams were getting to him again. Of course, he was still setting astounding records in all departments, but at the end of the season they were holding him to only three or four touchdowns a game, cutting his rushing average by some twenty-five percent, and intercepting a number of his passes, especially on the right flank, where he always thought he was strongest. He pushed deeper into the night with his thinking practice and risked cutting some of the foreplay and huddle techniques, but as a result he began showing other signs of strain. He lurched into a few wild plays in the last games and went offside a couple of times, knocked a Congresswoman's teeth out in a surprise body-block in her bathtub (she bit the cold-water tap as she came down), had an orgasm in a pileup on the field at which time some strange murmurings were also reported but not believed, and broke into a stream of abusive showerroom obscenities during a Quaker service in his honor at the Friends

Meeting House on the South Side, which nevertheless did not prevent him from seducing two of the ladies present and tackling a third."

"Like I'm telling you, Meyer, he was a kuntzen macher, like Harry says—you know, a real tricksmaker—I'm gonna miss him so . . ."

"Well, finally it was the Giants who broke him, in the championship game. They'd purchased a reserve Bear lineman surreptitiously by way of the Green Bay Packers in order to obtain firsthand intelligence about Gus's practice routines. At first this guy's information seemed useless: short on specifics about tactics and play patterns, long on apparent irrelevancies about spitting water and handholding and suchlike. They began to think the lineman himself was maybe a sleeper, a plant."

"Like those chazzers down at the steel plant who gave you all those bumps," she says, kissing the bruise on my shoulder, her hand stroking my thigh.

"Exactly, Golda. Some of the heavies on the Giants line even roughed the guy up a bit, but he stuck to his story. It was only about twenty-four hours before the playoff began that it suddenly occurred to them what it was all about. Their strategy the next day was to hit him at the fundamentals. They bribed the band to play "Roll Me Over in the Clover" instead of "The Star-Spangled Banner" during the opening ceremonies, so he didn't know whether to salute or sing along. When his linemen were bent over in front of him, they tossed him a wet towel."

"Ah . . . !" She touches her breast and, sighing, nods.

"They shouted out numbers when plays were being called, and by halftime had hit on '29' to make him go offside. They rushed offside themselves and hit him coming out of huddles just to confuse him. In pileups, they passed him condoms and blew in his ear, and once, when he succeeded in breaking free on a long run, they all stopped and applauded him. He pulled up, smiled, tossed the ball in the air, and jogged off the field toward the sidelines. The Bears recovered the ball that time, but the coach was in a state of absolute panic."

"What naughty tricks, Meyer!"

"Football's a rough game, Golda, especially when you're playing for money."

"It oughta be socialized . . ."

"There was worse to come. The Bears' coach had pulled Gus out of the game in the second quarter, but he couldn't win without him. So he drilled him intensely during the halftime break, a kind of short-hand run-through of the entire system, and sent him out for the second half, hoping for the best. For a few plays, he was okay. He went offside a couple of times on shouts of '29,' but he scored another touchdown on the old Statue of Liberty play, after making sixty-eight yards on two passes, one of them from behind his back, and a brilliant end run, and the Bears moved out in front by ten points. That was when the Giants played their sneaky ace in the hole. They had got ahold of one of the professionals Gus slept with for his nighttime sex drills and had suited her up. When the Bears got the ball again, the Giants brought her on. The Bear quarterback called a long downfield pass to Gus. Gus broke out of the huddle to see the girl standing behind the Giant line. He walked forward, going offside as the ball was snapped, and the Giants opened up to let him through. He was tilting his head just so—you can imagine . . ."

"Yes . . ."

"There was a flag down, but play continued as the Giants rushed the Bear quarterback. In desperation, he flung the ball at Gus's back: it struck him on the helmet just as he was snuggling in the girl's shoulderpads and she was unlacing his britches, caromed off into the arms of a waiting Giant, who lugged it all the way on a zigzag timekilling course to the Bears' seventeen-yard line before being brought down. Back in Giant territory, meanwhile, Gus was giving the packed stadium a show of his own. This was the girl he'd been using to practice the 'wheelbarrow,' 'windmill,' and 'buzzsaw' positions with, so the fans were treated to a lot of strenuous action, especially since they were both still tangled up somewhat in shoulderpads, cleats, and tattered jerseys."

"I think we done the wheelbarrow . . ."

"The referee was frantically signaling everything from illegal position and unsportsmanlike conduct to unnecessary roughness and intentional grounding, but Gus, deep into one of his fixed drills, was oblivious to everything but the sequence of procedures, and the girl—well, you know how the girls always got. The other players were too awestruck to interfere; it finally took the cops to break it up. And these guys were so agitated by what they saw—Gus's orgasm, when he got it off at last, sent the girl skidding on the icy field all the way into the endzone—that they went wild and clubbed the poor guy unmercifully. To make it worse, the band now struck up the National Anthem, and Gus stood up, saluted, and peed all over the cops just as they charged him. It was the worst beating since his father had whipped him with a razor strop for swimming in the railroad ditch in Yorba Linda. It was that and not the girl that broke him. Four years of tireless self-discipline, Golda, had come to this: the worst beating in his life. To a man like Gus, with no past and no future, such a beating is a kind of death: an unbearable, omnipresent moment. The intricate mechanism comes unglued—instead of a machine, all that's left is a bag of busted-up junk—and like with Humpty-

Dumpty, there's no way to put it back together again."

"It's sad, Meyer, his getting the business like that. Maybe that's what made him do what he did at the steel mill last Sunday. Because of the police, I mean . . ."

"Maybe. But I don't think so. He had no coherent memory of it that he could reflect upon, and he never would have understood why everybody was so mad that day, even if you had explained it to him. Nor could he think ahead to some kind of redress. The greatest lover and halfback in recent history—maybe of all time—was suddenly nothing, less than human, a kind of unwired puppet, unable even to recall his toilet training or his native language. The coach had a lot invested in him and tried to get him back on the old schedules, but there was nothing holding them together anymore. Some skills dwindled and disappeared, others became bizarrely exaggerated. He could still throw a football a country mile, but he couldn't receive, couldn't even catch a centered ball or take a hand-off. He had an erection night and day, but he couldn't find the place—any place— to stick it. He could still pinch bottoms on a crowded streetcar or feint through an entire enemy lineup, with or without the ball, but he was as likely to do both at the same time as to do neither. He could no longer tell the difference between a football

143

field, a crowded sidewalk, a bedroom, and a mad-house.

"Which of course was where they finally sent him—to a madhouse, I mean. They tried different ways to rehabilitate him. Psychoanalysis didn't work at all—it was like he didn't have any 'nor-malcy' to work back to. They experimented with courses he'd had in college, and he took a passing interest in history and government, but he could no longer get the hang of reading the pages con-secutively, so he developed a lot of weird and de-stabilizing ideas. They read in his file that he'd once played the piano, they tried that. He set about learning pieces one note at a time, but he was much slower now, it took him an entire day to learn a single bar, another day to learn a second, a whole week to put the two together. Still, it was better than nothing, and they kept at it, managing to get him all the way through 'The Curse of an Aching Heart' and halfway into 'Happy Days Are Here Again,' before he broke down again and started hauling the scores toward some imaginary endzone, trying to hump the grand piano, whis-pering sweet nothings into its soundbox. His mother, trying to help, reminded them about his old potato-mashing skills, but this got him even more mixed up. After the first night, the janitorial staff of the institution threatened to walk out if they ever had to clean up that kind of a mess again. At last somebody thought to try acting, he'd done a lot of that before, and this turned out to be the answer. Or anyway a kind of answer. They didn't cure him, but as an actor, his peculiar behavior seemed more acceptable, and some of his old routines could now be relearned as parts in a play. Once he had a repertoire established, they let him go, and not long after that he turned up here, that night you met him."

Golda sits thinking about this for a while, holding the bowl—now with just one strawberry left in it—pressed against her soft tummy and fleshy thighs. Finally, she sighs and says: "What if, Meyer . . . what if he was really, you know, a man ahead of his time?" Maybe, I think, staring out the hole Gus made in my partition into my silent dusty studio, I've been worrying too much about Maxim Gorky's eyes. Maybe I should have one of them wink, or cross them, or paint eyeballs on cardboard that can be moved from side to side and up and down behind the cavities. "Like, maybe, if we had only given him more love and understanding, this woulda never happened . . ."

"Maybe that's what we're all dying of, Golda. Love and understanding . . ."

"Not me," she replies brightly and claps a hand on my leg. "Here, Meyer," she grins, plucking the last strawberry from the bowl with her free hand, and pinching my own hand, still between her legs, "this'll cure the alienation what ails you!" I lean forward to suck it from her fingers, but she drops it down her cleft, poking it deep inside the brassiere. "Communism don't deprive any man of the power to appropriate the products of society," she lectures huskily, sliding her hand up my thigh, "but you got to show you got a appetite . . ."

And that's how it happens that I've got my nose deep in Golda's brassiere, her hand yanking on my stiffened organ, when her brother Harry comes in with Jesse, carrying Ilya between them, out cold, along with some other guys I never saw before, all boisterously singing "Raggedy, Raggedy Are We." When they see us like that, they switch to "Nekkid, nekkid are we . . . !" Left it open again . . . yet again. Well . . . as long as I've got my nose in there, I figure I might as well get what I came for.

"Say, we seen all them pretty flowers on the door," Jesse declares, as they dump Ilya on some tarps in a corner. They've got some bottles as well, a sack of potatoes, and a peeled bird. "You guys celebratin' the Duke losin' his cherry or somethin'?"

I come up with the strawberry between my teeth, and one of the newcomers says: "Naw, he's jist bobbin' fer apples!"

"Who said they was no free lunch?"

They all roar with drunken laughter and Jesse says: "Hey, let's sing 'em your weddin' song, Harry! C'mon, Billy Dean!"

Golda flushes politely and pulls on her clothes, muttering something about going out to see if my pants are dry ("I was afraid he'd catch his death of cold, Harry!"), while the others spread their feet apart to keep from tipping over, wrap their arms around each other's shoulders, and bellow forth (the tune might be "Yankee Doodle," but probably isn't):

> *"Jolly old Wally*
> *Said to Eddie*
> *In their wedding bed:*
> *'Where've you kept*
> *That great big scepter*
> *You had before we wed?'*

> *"Said Ed to Wally:*
> *'I'm so solly,*
> *If you are frustrated,*
> *But this thing,' he said,*
> *'Between us is dead,*
> *I've been expropriated!'"*

"They're still wet," says my Homecoming Queen when she comes back in. The others are all hoo-haing, snorting, slapping their knees, genuinely

147

pleased with themselves. In the midst of it all, Golda and I are introduced to Billy Dean and his friends Gordon and Elroy, Jesse explaining in a loud voice that they all need a place to bunk down for a couple of nights and that Gordon, who's said to be a painter and hopeful of getting on some WPA arts project now that he's heard about them, is staying with me.

"And lookie here," says Jesse, holding up the scraggly bird, "we found this here kosher chicken on the way up, jist layin' there—musta got hit by a damn car!"

"Probably it committed suicide," booms Harry, "caught out there in that kuckamaimie without its feathers on!"

"Now howzabout conjurin' up somethin' clever with the remains, Goldie, so's the pore cock won'ta died in vain?"

"Well," she says, glancing at me, "if it's all right with Meyer . . ."

"Sure, it's all right with Meyer," snorts Harry. "If he don't eat nothing but strawberries, he'll get the f'kucken scurvy!"

"I thought berries was supposed to be good for scurvy," says Golda.

"Well, scabies, then. Or diabetes. Whatever it is, it is sure to be the end of the little petseleh, if not worse!"

"There's some fish, too," I say, tired of my own silence. "A red mullet."

"I knowed I smelt somethin' dreadful," says one of the newcomers.

"Now, that's a very poetical and appetizin' combynation!" exclaims Jesse, slapping the lump of yellowish chicken flesh down on the table. "Mullet 'n pullet!"

"Don't talk dirty, Jesse," Golda scolds, poking through my toolbox for a usable knife.

"Hey, did you hear, Meyer?" Harry says. "General Mola is dead! The old shitser crashed in a airplane today!"

"Man, that nigger cat sure got a style for disassemblin' a fishhead!" groans the one called Billy Dean, watching the Baron at work. "Kinda takes your appetite away . . ."

"If something happens to f'kucken Franco now, chavairim, the whole shitpot could break down!" says Harry cheerfully, his fat cheeks piled back toward his ears in a mirthless grin. "Things could be maybe better in Spain after all this than they ever were!"

Hasn't he seen what's happening, I wonder. ("Dam' right, Harry!" says Jesse, uncapping a bottle of Silver Dollar whiskey.) Maybe not. Some things we just don't want to know. Elroy switches the radio on and tunes in *The Lone Ranger*.

"Man, lookit this thang! Somebody been usin' this raddio for *target* practice!"

"Billy Dean here knows a guy who was down at Republic Sunday," Jesse says, throwing a wink my way. "He says the first shots probably come from inside . . ."

Billy Dean stammers something defensive about this unnamed friend being on the wrong side, not knowing what was really going on, but that he learned his lesson watching how the police worked that day. His version of Gloomy Gus's charge: "He seemed to be blowin' smoke outa his butt, like somebody dropped somethin' in his pants!" Harry by now is completely convinced that Gus was a police informer and that the story of his rehabilitation after he crashed out of professional football was just an elaborate fabrication to cover the time of his police training. Golda says she doesn't think any of the political theories are correct, nor does she buy the idea that he was just a freakish psychopath that Leo manipulated or was manipulated by. She thinks he was an ordinary man of ordinary abilities possessed by an heroic vision of life. He'd sacrificed a lot of things most people take as normal—including normal social behavior—in his effort to realize that vision, with the consequences that, like many geniuses (here she glances my way winsomely), when he achieved his goal the ordinary people he'd once been a part of couldn't understand him anymore. He knew this, and so when his moment came he gave, not explanations or advice, but himself. "Like a poet . . ."

I smile. One of my figures of a dancer has fallen—maybe it fell a month ago when I got hit by Guernica—and I see that it looks interesting on its side like that. Like somebody twisting to be free of chains. I realize suddenly that what I want to do is make sculptures that reveal different things at the same time, have profiles substantially different and a number of uniquely meaningful positions. O.B. arrives while I'm thinking about this (what does it have to do with my idea about dissonance, I wonder), and says he heard that Gus had captured the Republic Steel plant single-handed Sunday and had got shot singing "Happy Days Are Here Again" from the plant roof. There are some awkward moments as the Southern boys shy from this hardy black man, but they're soon got over through O.B.'s own good nature and Jesse's embracing sympathies, Jesse informing them all that he's got a new song called "Whatever Happened to Gloomy Gus?" O.B. is more or less on his way to Mad-hatten, as he calls it, but says he needs a corner to sack out in for a couple of nights while he winds down his local love life, and can he stay here? He seems unusually gregarious and self-confident, but I can see that underneath the heartiness he's frightened, so I can't say no.

I'm beginning to feel ill at ease sitting around in that crowd in my underwear, so I go outside for my pants. They're still damp, but I pull them on anyway—like Gus said: "One has to be uncomfortable to do one's best thinking." What I'm thinking about is how to cut a swath through all these friends, the impinging news mosaic, swastikas and wedding feasts, all my new ideas for projects, and the "cold oily bubble" of life itself, in order to get back to Maxim Gorky's eyes. No way, probably. The invitation is out as it has always been. Friends will come. The Condor Legion will come. Ideas, too, like dust motes in the afternoon. It's a kind of cranial erosion, a Dust Bowl of the mind. I'm excited by that notion of multifaceted pieces, it's even better than the one I had earlier about polarities and confrontations, and I'm eager to light the torch before it all gets away from me, but . . . not quite eager enough.

I stand outside for a few minutes (can't stay as long as I might like: it's starting to sprinkle again), feeling the iron railroad spikes in my pocket, lying heavily, wet and cold, against my leg, and gazing in on my friends through the back door. Jesse is tuning up his guitar, his long bony knees stuck out in the small room like angle irons. Harry is peeling potatoes for his sister Golda at the sink, squinting closely at them through his thick lenses. O.B. and Billy Dean are trading down-home stories, and the Baron is in O.B.'s lap getting his ears scrubbed. O.B. never liked cats until he started hanging around this place and took to the Baron. In fact he helped name him, as we went from Charlie the Tramp (his peculiar walk after being hit by a car) to radio's Baron ("Wass you dere, Sharlie?") Munchausen to simply the Baron ("That cat ain't no tramp!" O.B. declared with a brotherly grin) and finally the Black Baron, referring more to his banner than to his color ("What I don't like about cats," Leo had said, "is you can't organize them!"). Ilya is awake and throwing up in the bucket I keep my metal scraps for Maxim Gorky in, but that's all right, it'll wash out. And Gorky won't care, being accustomed to our self-destructions and—who knows—maybe even in the end admiring them.

Gloomy Gus, before he died, became a little delirious and mistook me for his coach back at Whittier College. He apparently understood that the trouble was he'd gone offside again, and he was apologizing for letting the team down. "Try to forget about it, Gus," I said. "The game's not over yet."

"Chief," he whispered, tears forming in the corners of his eyes (was this another act, I wondered, had I thrown him another cue?), "why is it we go on forever, making the first mistake we ever made . . . over and over again?"

I knew the answer, but I didn't think he really wanted to know. He looked genuinely anguished, but with Gloomy Gus this didn't mean a thing. "Well, it's probably *not* a mistake, Gus," I said finally. "Probably it's only—"

But by then he was dead.

About the Author

Robert Coover was born in Iowa in 1932. His first novel, *The Origin of the Brunists,* was the winner of the 1966 William Faulkner Award. His other works include *The Universal Baseball Association, J. Henry Waugh, Prop.; Pricksongs & Descants; A Theological Position; The Public Burning; A Political Fable; Spanking the Maid; Gerald's Party;* and *A Night at the Movies.* Coover lives with his wife, Pili, in Providence, Rhode Island, where he teaches at Brown University.